Hemophobia

Also by Donald Healey

Gods of Rain and Blood

The Road to Glorieta; a Confederate Army Marches through New Mexico

Boomers Away; Travels at the Edge of the Comfort Zone

Puffernut Flies South

The Bequest

Hemophobia

Donald Healey

Granite Mountain Books, LLC

Prescott, AZ

Copyright © 2023 Donald Healey

Library of Congress Control Number:

2024901243

Published by: Granite Mountain Books, LLC

Prescott, AZ 86301

ISBN: 979-8-9890538-8-9

Contents

Chapter 1

The lucky number eleven bus puffed out what sounded like an expectant sigh and its well-oiled front door slid smoothly open. Clarita Jackson stepped off the curb, wrestled with two unwieldly mesh shopping bags and heaved her considerable bulk aboard. "Good evening, Gideon," she smiled.

"Why, good evening to you too, Miz Jackson!" responded the uniformed driver. Gideon loved driving the number eleven, especially at night. On most routes, night was when the crazies came out, but not on good old number eleven. On the eleven, it was regular people getting off the late shift, normal friendly people like missus Jackson. Gideon looked at her bags and then glanced at his other five passengers. Nobody appeared rushed. "Hey Clarita," he offered. "You want me to help you get to your seat with those bags?"

"Gideon Robinson," she grunted, "how long have I been riding your bus? Have I ever needed your help with my bags? Just close the door and drive me on home to my children."

"Yes, Mam," grinned Gideon, "but I know how many kids you've got at home, and neither of us is getting any younger." Laughing to himself, he shut the door and pulled his bus away from the curb.

Gideon was forty-seven, and he'd been driving nights for the MBTA since he was twenty-eight. For fifteen of those years he'd driven the night shift on the number eleven. For fourteen of them, as regular as clockwork, Clarita Jackson had stood at her stop, pass in hand, waiting to climb aboard. When they were both younger, before all her kids, they used to flirt. Now, they enjoyed a sort of tongue in cheek one-that-got-away friendship.

Approaching the corner of A Street and Wormwood, Gideon spied a shadow waiting in the designated stop enclosure. The door of his bus once again hissed open. He waited, but the only thing that came up the eleven's steps was a sudden goose-bump-raising gust of cold air. The passenger was nowhere in sight. In his mirror, his six passengers were looking forward at him with quizzical expressions. Gideon shrugged. *Hell that was strange.* It wasn't often that he made that sort of blunder.

As the eleven rumbled back into light traffic, he again used his mirror to quickly check on his passengers. That glimpse sent an icy shiver down his spine. There was a man, a that man he hadn't seen before, and the man was staring intently at Gideon from two rows behind Clarita.

How did that asshole get onboard? he questioned. He knew that he hadn't scanned the man's pass and he also knew that the man hadn't paid cash. In fact, he was sure that the man had never even walked past him.

The stranger, perhaps thirty, was blond, handsome, and very well dressed. Just seeing him made Gideon nearly swerve and slam on his brakes.

In the minutes that followed, the bus crawled along and his eyes kept returning to the mirror. With each glance, his confusion slowly gave way to a nameless dread. *Lord protect me,* he thought, *that man, that man is evil!*

Gideon wasn't a church-goer, but he believed in God and he considered himself pious in his own relaxed way. The unexpected passenger seemed to drag claws through the very core of his fragile faith. Like the sound of nails on a blackboard, the feeling couldn't be ignored. The man engendered in the congenial bus driver a visceral upwelling of spiritual fear and revulsion. The sensation was unlike anything that he'd ever experienced.

What the hell? shivered Gideon. *He's just another passenger.* Coinciding with this thought, the man pressed the button to request a stop. Shivering, Gideon directed his bus over to the curb at the corner with Cypher Street. Filled with loathing, he opened the door and watched as the blond stranger strode past him and descended. Grateful, Gideon started to close the door when the man abruptly hesitated and looked back with piercing blue-white eyes.

"Thank you, Gideon," he hissed. "Whatever happens next, that's all on you!"

Stunned, Gideon watched in mute silence as the man strolled nonchalantly away. He felt a strange pull, then he jerked to his feet. His other passengers stared at him; puzzlement clearly written on all six of their faces.

"I have to," he moaned.

The man wasn't a man. He couldn't say how, but Gideon knew with absolute certainty that the passenger was something else, a demon, and an incarnation of purest evil. Unless someone stopped the creature, it was going do unspeakable things. Gideon stared at the retreating figure. Suddenly, he understood the reason that he alone had seen the monster. God was offering him a cross to bear.

"What the hell, Gideon?" shouted one of his regular passengers as the reliable driver lurched away from his seat.

"What's happening? Where you going?" yelled another.

"Gideon, are you all right?" worried Clarita.

Without an answer, or even a single backward look, Gideon leapt from the door of the idling number eleven and jogged off down the street.

At forty-seven, six two and 225 pounds, he was still in good shape, but the demon was quick and it was wily. Although the thing never seemed to hurry, it always managed to stay, tantalizingly, just out of reach. It glided effortlessly down this street and up that alley. It hopped onto the Red Line and then moved from one subway circuit to another. Gideon always knew where it was, but he never managed to get any closer. It was playing with him.

Just before dawn, Gideon gave up his fruitless chase. Upset, muddled, and thoroughly exhausted, he hailed a yellow cab to take him back to his tiny apartment. Inside, he bolted the door, removed his jacket, and threw himself onto his bed, not bothering to pull back its covers.

When he awoke the next day, groggy and tired, he still sensed the demon. It was just ahead of him and he could almost hear its laughter. Tired though he was, he knew what had to be done. He got down on his knees beside his bed and began an earnest rambling prayer to a God with whom he rarely spoke. At length, certain that he'd been heard and chosen, he climbed back to his feet. He grabbed a duffel, quickly stuffed it with his spare uniform, underwear, and socks. Then, he strode purposefully out of his apartment door. This time, he didn't trouble to lock it. Gideon knew that he was never coming back.

Fate, capricious and inexorable, had snatched him out of his comfortable life and thrust him into some sort of vicious game. The demon existed. He'd seen it. Now, he had to stop it. God had left him no other choice.

Resolutely, he shouldered his duffle, walked to the corner and waited. As sure as a lighted signpost beckoning in the distance, he felt evil's pull. With a weighty sense of purpose and of impending destiny, Gideon turned west and began to walk.

Chapter 2

Parched dry prairie stretched out on both sides of the old ribbon of cracked asphalt. Nothing except wilted grasses and pitiful bits of sage, nothing out there offered the man a place to rest his eyes. Sunset held its promise in the distance, but shimmers of oven-like heat still glimmered above the baked pavement.

The man existed like an extension of the prairie, a dried out echo of once vibrant life, worn-down, stretched thin, and bleached of color. One or two cars had passed him that day. Despite the sweltering heat, none had stopped. None had even slowed. None offered a ride.

"Will you look at that, Helen," the man in the green pickup had grunted to his wife, "another goddamn shabby transient, and a black one at that!"

If the couple had cared to look more closely, they might have noticed that although the man was threadbare, he wasn't truly unkempt. Over a dress shirt, that had once been a brighter shade of white, and a clip-on tie, he wore a short-waist two-pocket jacket with a large shiny silver snap on each of the flaps. Bright red piping once accented the two pockets, but now it was just piping, any of its original color a distant memory. An American flag patch sat affixed to the jacket's left shoulder. On its right shoulder a round embroidered patch featuring a large letter "T" filled the same space. A baseball cap with a stenciled version of the same "T" logo printed in white above a line of five large numbers protected the man's head. Like the piping, the patches and the hat were badly faded and shifting slowly toward invisibility. His pants, once heavy duty work slacks, still evidenced the ghosts of creases down their front. His feet were laced into high-top shoes that started their life as waterproof duty boots.

The whole grayish ensemble, which may have once been dark blue, was much too warm for such a day. Except for another outfit just like it, some socks and a change of underwear, it was all the clothes the man owned. In his left hand he clutched an old ratty duffle bag. In his right he carried a long case for a pool cue or maybe a musical instrument.

In contrast to the rest of the faded man's appearance, the case was elegant. His shoes were starting to come apart and sometimes that worried the man.

He wasn't sure where he was. *Maybe somewhere in eastern Oregon?* suggested his inner voice. He clearly remembered Gatesville, Texas, but he'd walked for more than two years since leaving that place. His life was like that. Sometimes he'd come to himself, walking along a highway, and just be someplace different, no idea where, and no idea how he got there.

Where he needed to go next was another matter. God made sure he knew. He always felt the pull. And, the pull was always stronger when he drew closer. The pull was strong today.

He'd again caught up with the evil one in Gatesville, but not in time to put a stop to him, not before the demon subverted more innocents. Just as he had done each time before, the creature then simply disappeared and left the man to deal with the abominations that he'd created. *The demon feeds on the living and infects those from whom it feeds.*

A dry unpleasant wind pushed at his back, a prickly thing that carried no moisture and hinted of ill tidings. Even though he was still too hot, it made the man tug at his jacket and hug it tighter. The wind bent the dead prairie grass and blew a bit of trash past his feet. As he watched the moving trash dance in tiny circles, a metallic clatter interrupted his fugue and made him look up. The spiteful wind gusted and a rusted green metal sign rattled on its pole. "Pickle's Forge, alt. 1,385, pop. 1023, Green River Ord. Enforced"

A few miles farther down the deserted road the man could, by shading his eyes, just make out wide swaths of green, leafy trees, and a small low-lying town. Lights had yet to come on and the town's buildings presented dark featureless outlines against the setting sun. The man couldn't tell what the small community might offer; nevertheless, its proximity brought a brief smile to his weathered face.

That place is probably big enough to have a diner. It could even have a motel, he mused. He reached into a zippered pants pocket and withdrew a roll of bills. In another life the man had been frugal. He couldn't remember the last time that he had accessed an ATM and dipped into his savings, but the roll from his pocket was still thick. *It'll do*, he thought, *maybe tonight I'll get a shower and sleep in a bed.*

It was well after dark when he reached a rural highway junction about a half mile out from the town. Crossing the road, he plodded past The States Motel's flickering neon sign and stepped into its tiny office. Behind the Formica counter, a pimply adolescent night clerk sat reading a comic book and picking at his nose. When the man walked in, he took his finger away from his snout and dropped the comic.

"Hey, what do you want?" His voice sounded a little high, maybe tinged with a bit of puberty or fear.

"You're a motel, right?" asked the man. "I'd like a room for three nights."

"They're $25 a night," mumbled the clerk, "but you gotta have an ID and a credit card."

"I don't have either," sighed the man, pulling his roll from his wallet, "but I do have cash." He peeled a Benjamin off the roll and placed it in front of the boy. "How's about I pay you $30 a night for your inconvenience and you keep the change?"

A cagy look slid across the young clerk's face and he reached behind him for a key. "Sure we can do that. Just sign this register and you can take number eight, out the door and to your left."

"Thank you," said the man. "Anywhere around here to get a warm bite to eat?"

"Naw," replied the clerk glancing at his watch and picking his comic back up, "too late. Café closes early on Friday, but there's a vending machine next to number five."

The name on the States Motel's register read, "Joe Smith." The man knew from long experience that when you paid cash small places never bothered to look.

Chapter 3

If you don't want to sit out on your porch and listen to the crickets or sit inside and watch reruns of Jeopardy, the nightlife available in Pickle's Forge offers exactly two options. If you're of the older male persuasion, you head over to the Elks-Lodge-cum-Vets'-Club, shoot the shit with your buddies, and then settle in for some serious drinking. If, on the other hand, you are a pair of feisty young women like Jane Carhill and Marybeth Barger, you wriggle into your tightest jeans and your sexiest halter-tops. Then you stroll over to the Sidle Inn where young men will buy you drinks and twirl you around the sawdust strewed floor to the scratchy tunes of the joint's ancient jukebox.

Arm-in-arm and laughing, Jane and Marybeth pushed open the Sidle Inn's front door and stepped out into its gravel parking lot. As Friday nights go in Pickle's Forge, it was a good one. They'd both flirted, danced, and drunk their fill, and it hadn't cost either of them a dime. It was only a little after midnight and raucous sounds of the old jukebox, rowdy conversation, and cigarette smoke trailed them outside. The revelry was still going strong, but over the years Jane's momma had told them time and again, "Leave the party while you're still having fun!" A little more than tipsy, and with hangovers just another drink or two away, it seemed a good time to heed her advice.

As they swayed for a moment enjoying the clean air that was just shedding the worst of the day's heat, the door swung open behind them. Turning to the renewed flood of sound, they faced Bobby Earl, holding a long-neck beer and leaning self-confidently against the jamb.

Bobby was lean and tall and he worked as a modern-day cowboy over at the Lazy B Ranch. On nights out, he milked the part for all it was worth. He sported an expensive black Stetson Skyline cowboy hat and his polished boots were Tecovas Caimans. His tailored cowboy shirt was silk, carefully embroidered, and it sparkled with mother of pearl buttons. A belt with a large silver buckle cinched his like-new Levis in tight at his waist.

"Aw come on Marybeth, don't go," he pleaded. "The night's still young." He'd been hovering around the two girls all night like a moth to a flame.

"Nope! No way, we're outta here, Bobby. I've had my fill of honky-tonk sweet talk for one night."

"If you stay, I'll buy the next round."

"Oh come on," wheedled Jane. "Bobby's real cute, and he's offering to buy again."

"Oh yeah, like you really need another beer," laughed Marybeth. Taking a firm hold on Jane's shoulders, she turned her friend around and started to lead her away.

"If you won't stay, how's about I drive you home?" shouted Bobby. "It's not right for two fine princesses like yourselves to have to be walking."

"Forget it Bobby Earl," shouted back Marybeth. "You put your silver tongue away. I ain't no Goldilocks and Janie ain't no Red Riding Hood and, you ain't getting lucky tonight!"

As Jane and Marybeth sashayed unsteadily away, Bobby took a long swig of his beer. "Now that there, that's a crying shame," he lamented, and strolled back inside. Behind him, the door slammed shut with a loud bang, a bang which no one inside heard over Merle Haggard belting out "Big City" from the jukebox.

Away from the lights of the bar, the night grew dark and the normal night sounds withered into an unsettling silence. Marybeth and Jane had walked home from the Sidle Inn at least a hundred times since high school, but tonight something felt different.

"Marybeth, I'm scared," gulped Jane.

"Jeezus, Jane, you're not scared, you're drunk," giggled Marybeth.

"No seriously, I think someone's following us."

"Oh, bullshit, Janie! If anyone's out here, it's just Bobby Earl, still thinking with his pecker."

"It ain't Bobby Earl, and I'm real scared."

"Okay then, let's get you home." Marybeth took Jane's hand and, by unspoken consensus, their wobbly pace increased.

Silence around them grew deeper and unnerving minutes crept by. They were alone; the gravel on the shoulder of the lane crunched under their feet. Then, out of nowhere, the man was just there. He stood stock still and silent in the middle of the road. A single stray ray of moonlight filtered down through the trees, but it wasn't enough to make the dark man visible or to pick out his features. What felt almost visible was an eddying vortex of menace that seemed to swirl about him.

"What the fuck do you want, asshole?" shrilled Marybeth.

The man leapt forward with uncanny speed and suddenly Jane was alone. Her childhood friend, Marybeth, lay, seemingly dead, on the pavement. Shocked and terrified, Jane screamed and plunged away from the road. Her mind descended to some reptilian level and she simply ran. Branches scratched at her face. She panted. She tripped. She fled through the trees, driven onward by the rule of unreasoning panic.

Crashing sounds of pursuit drew closer and she looked frantically over her shoulder. Her breath came in gasps. Then, just in front of her loomed an old tin-roofed woodshed. Stripped of rational thought, she threw herself inside and yanked closed its rickety leather-hinged door.

Except for clouds of clinging cobwebs, two forgotten logs, and a moldering pile of burlap bags, the old shed was empty. *911!* shrieked an animal part of her brain. *911!* She reached for the rhinestone-studded phone in her back pocket. *Nothing! My pocket's empty! Lost! Oh God! Oh Fuck!* Stifling a terrified sob, Jane hunkered into a corner and tried to make herself as small as possible. Her breath rushed in and out as loud rasping gasps and she threw her hands over her face to stifle the noise.

Outside the shed, someone scratched at the door. "Little pig, little pig, let me in; let me in."

Jane whimpered.

Another scratch at the door, "My, what big ears I have."

Jane tried to squeeze herself further into the corner. She quivered. The door slowly twisted open and moonlight framed a looming figure. She knew it was the man from the road, but he was still just a black silhouette, a monster devoid of features.

"My, what big eyes I have. I see you," he whispered.

Bright red animal eyes seemed to glow in the silhouette's face and Jane Carhill screamed, and screamed again.

Back at the Sidle Inn, Bobby Earl settled his bill and, with a self-satisfied look, swaggered out its door with Cindy Munson clutched tightly onto his arm.

Chapter 4

Although it was still before 8 am, Saturday was shaping up to be a real scorcher. Andy Cates, dressed in patched overalls, a long-sleeved faded-blue work shirt, and a Spokane Indians baseball cap carefully threaded his way through towering stalks of corn, heavy with ears and nearly ready for harvest. In front of him, carefully pointed toward the ground, he carried a Stoeger "Uplander," shotgun. The youth model, double-barreled .410 was a gift for his thirteenth birthday two days earlier. Young Andy hadn't had a chance to fire the weapon yet, but he planned to rectify that situation real soon.

Also dressed in overalls, but carrying an off-brand single-shot .22 rifle, his best friend, Larry "Coop" Cooper, followed at a safe distance. "Hey, Andy, whadda ya say we call it quits?" he yawned. "I'm bored and it's getting way too hot. Let's go on home."

"No way, Coop!" objected Andy. "I haven't had a chance to try this baby out. I'm not ready yet."

"Well I am," grumbled Coop, pulling off his own cap and wiping sweat from his eyes. "We've been at this stupid hunt since daybreak and ain't neither of us shot nothing."

"You go if you wanta go. I'm gonna keep hunting."

Coop was two years older than Andy, and kind of viewed him as a fun, but often annoying, younger brother. He wasn't about to leave him wandering around by himself with his new shotgun. "Aw come on Andy, you're just being stubborn. This is a waste of time."

"Quiet!" murmured Andy.

Coop didn't like to be shushed, but then he heard the rustle of quail scurrying through the corn. Both boys looked at each other and smiled. Andy placed a finger to his lips in the universal sign for silence and then pointed among the stalks. Coop saw a flicker of movement and nodded. Treading with all the stealth they could muster the boys struck out in pursuit. After about fifty yards, they slowed to a halt. The rustling had gone silent and nothing around them moved.

"Beans!" grumbled Andy. Then, Coop again heard something.

"Shssh," he whispered. "They're over this way." Turning away from his younger companion, he raised his rifle and pushed against a thick screen of corn. Without warning the sturdy-looking stalks, unexpectedly, gave way. Coop flailed and tried to catch himself, but his efforts were futile. Stumbling over his own feet, he crashed loudly into an open space, and landed on his knees.

Pandemonium greeted his arrival. Piercing squawks and screeching assaulted his ears, and wings battered at his head as hundreds of large startled crows exploded into the sky.

"Coop? Coop are you alright?" shouted Andy.

"Sure, just feeling really stupid," he grinned and twisted toward his friend.

The younger boy's expression wiped away the grin. Andy shook, his eyes were the size of saucers, and all the color was draining from his face. Whipping back around, Coop stared for a moment. Next, he dropped to all fours and emptied his stomach.

Stretched out in the middle of a flattened circle of corn, like some madman's parody of Christ on his cross, lay the crucified body of a young woman. Huge iron nails pinned her lifeless hands and feet to the ground and a puddle of dried blood attested to the savagery of the stab wound in her side. Her severed head lay on its side and its eyeless sockets stared emptily at the two boys and spoke to them of the legions of nightmares yet to come.

Chapter 5

Portland's FBI field office building stands four stories tall, a huge presence all about sharp angles and mirrored windows, somebody's off-base idea of understated modern. Kitrina Kathleen Butters, "Mickey" to her friends, had only been there for two weeks and already she hated the place. Today was worse than usual. In the wake of a national calamity, the field office had transformed itself into a maddened hornets' nest of activity.

Still an hour or two before dawn's first light, somber men and stone-faced women rushed about hither and thither, dressed in their dark suits and shiny shoes, or sporting pressed jeans and iconic black windbreakers stenciled with "FBI." Some of the men and some of women hurried about empty-handed. Others clutched file folders or carried enigmatic cardboard boxes that were taped firmly shut. Every one of them looked serious enough to be on a personally assigned mission from God.

With the exception of Mickey's own phones, every other communication device in the whole building seemed to vie for attention, generating an incessant low-level cacophony of annoying buzzes and chimes. On a wall twenty-feet away from her desk, a large-screen display-panel was tuned to FOX News. The Fox commentators sounded excited to the point of orgasm as various scenes of destruction repeated themselves above screaming banners. A pair of special agents paused near Mickey's desk to watch.

"Five field offices at once! Dear God what a nightmare!" extolled the blond.

"Salt Lake, Seattle, San Francisco, Sacramento, LA; why weren't we hit here in Portland?" wondered his Latino partner. Mickey didn't know either of the men.

"Maybe they tried. Maybe it just didn't go off. Looks like they tried for all the field offices on the West Coast."

"Damn good try I'd say. Your stupid rabbit's foot musta been working overtime this morning." Mickey watched as the blond agent pull the key-chained foot of some unfortunate white rabbit out of his pants pocket, and self-consciously held it in his fist.

"That leaves just us and San Diego. I think we're in for some serious overtime, Amigo." Reluctantly breaking contact with the screen, the two men stalked off to attend to whatever important tasks they'd been assigned.

Mickey looked around the room and sighed quietly. *I'm not supposed to be here*, she thought. That wasn't exactly true. She had dreamed of being in the FBI ever since she was twelve. She blamed her ambition to join that specific security force on Special Agent Mavis Peterson. Peterson, at the time one of the agency's few female agents, was the shining star of an assembly at Mickey's middle school. By the time Mavis finished waving her flag and extoling the agency's virtues, Mickey had known with the absolute unshakeable certainty of an impressionable tween that the FBI was the only career for her.

Now, here she sat in Portland, a newly-minted special agent herself, doing absolutely nothing while chaos swirled around her. It wasn't that she no longer wanted to be part of the agency; it was just that her present situation was demanding a drastically lowered set of expectations.

Mickey had graduated from high school two years early and had immediately moved on to a good university where she majored in cyber security and criminology. Working day and night, she'd left academia four years later, still a virgin but holding both a B.S. and an M.S. degree. Since her instructors and peers alike all considered her something of a wunderkind, Mickey immediately received multiple offers of employment. Her acceptance nod went to LockCell, a small but widely-respected cyber-security business. Later, after two fruitful years in the private sector, she reached the ripe old age of twenty-three. With one disastrous affair, her virginity, and all of the agency's prerequisites behind her, Mickey immediately applied to the FBI. Everything went according to her plan until it came time for her Physical Fitness Test.

The PFT requires potential candidates to demonstrate prowess in five events: sit-ups for maximum reps in one minute, a timed 300-meter sprint, pushups done for maximum reps, a timed

1.5-mile run, and pullups for maximum reps. Mickey, who never gave much thought to physical fitness, failed miserably. At home in her apartment, she'd cried, she beat her fists against the wall. She wallowed in depression.

At that low-point, she took a good long look at herself in the mirror. Over the years, friends had unsurprisingly flattered Mickey for her personality rather than her physical traits. Her height was a little below average and her pageboy hair tended toward a mousey brown. Her facial features, while not striking, did come together pleasantly, giving her sort of an endearing girl-next-door look. She'd always thought of her waist as a little thick and her butt a little wide, but she'd been okay with that. Standing in front of the unforgiving mirror, she had to admit that things weren't at their best. Her two years at LockCell palling around with other uber-nerds and living on Dr. Pepper and Hot Pockets had not been kind. She'd definitely put on weight and lost most of her muscle.

Well crap! Double crap! she thought. *Either I just drop out right now, or I woman-up and get back in shape.* Mickey knew that there was truly only one choice, so she took it. She ran. She pumped iron at the gym. She watched what she ate. She lost weight. Then, two months later, exuding a deep confidence in her new-found level of fitness, she promptly failed her second PFT.

The test required that she earn at least twelve points with at least one point in three events, and no points less than a zero in any event. Mickey managed to accumulate ten points, but she'd received a negative score on her pullups. Once again weepy, but knowing that she would only get one more try, she redoubled her efforts. It was either pass her third and final PFT or give up her closely-held dreams of the FBI.

Failure was never an option. So, on a Thursday morning another month later, Mickey squeaked by. She ran the fastest 300 meters of her life adding one point to her previous best. Going into pullups, her score was still short, but straining, groaning, and clenching her teeth she managed to eke out one point, pushing her total up to the magic number twelve.

After that, Mickey was back in the pipe five by five. As expected, she received an offer of appointment to the FBI contingent on her passing a thorough and rigorous background investigation. As she also expected, the investigation approved her with flying colors.

Her polygraph test yielded some uncertain results, and also a few uncomfortable moments. Luckily, however, since she was never asked any questions about the one thing that was truly problematic, the machine never accused her of lying. The examiner frowned at what he saw. Still, it was the end of a long day. He looked at the clock in his office, shrugged his shoulders, and wrote off her tiny anomalies as first-time lie detector jitters.

Next, it was back to school for an 800 hour, nineteen-week "Basic Field Training Course." Finally, upon graduation, Kitrina Kathleen Butters was duly sworn in as a genuine FBI special agent, bringing her dream to fruition. Portland was her first posting. *Pacific Northwest, here I come!*

The moment when she walked in for her first real day on the job was the instant when her need for lowered expectations suddenly arose. For some reason the Portland field office wasn't even expecting her! The greetings she received were polite, then, like a hot potato, she was quickly passed from one person to another. Every person, who she was assured was the "right" person, seemed unsure what to do with her. In response, she dutifully presented each individual with her paperwork and carefully explained that she was being assigned to the Portland field office's cyber-crimes unit. That information invariably elicited a look of sympathy or confusion.

The person who finally took her under her wing, was Mable Wilson. Mable was a veteran non-agent staff employee who served as the huge building's third-floor office manager.

"Listen Hon," she sympathized, "everyone understands that you're supposed to work in the cyber unit. It's just that there isn't any room."

"What do you mean, there isn't any room?" asked Mickey, who was by this time more than a little confused.

"You see, our cyber unit is way down in the basement and it's just plain packed to its gills," answered Mable. "The space down there was built for storage, not computers. Now, between equipment and personnel, it's bursting its ancient red brick seams. Right now at least, there's just not enough room to even shoehorn you in."

Well shit! "So what am I supposed to do?" frowned Mickey.

"Don't worry Hon, I'll find you a cozy space right here on third and I'll make sure that your real department knows that you're here."

And, that's how Mickey ended up at a standard secretarial desk with a couple of shitty lo-res monitors and no access to anything remotely useful to her supposed position.

"Nope unh-uh," a sympathetic network technician told her. "There's no connection between the rest of the building and the systems in the basement; it's way too sensitive down there to allow any access."

Mickey was invited to a couple of departmental staff meetings with her future co-workers, but to a man they greeted her with doubt and skepticism. The boys in the basement, and they were all "boys," were protective of their crowded territory. Even her official boss-to-be, Frank Guinn, acted like she was an unwanted imposition. Left to gnash her teeth and curse under her breath, Mickey was forced to admit that she was effectively out of the cyber-crimes loop. For that matter, as best she could determine, she was out of all the loops.

When she'd last checked 23.5 percent of FBI special agents were female. The agency loudly and vociferously professed its deep commitment to diversity and made a particular point that the 23.5 percent were superb agents who just happened to be women. From what Mickey had experienced so far, she was pretty sure that someone in the Portland field office had missed that particular memo.

The approach of Steve Smallwood, Portland's local agent in charge, made her sit up straight and try to look engaged. She'd only met Smallwood once when he mistook her for an office assistant and asked her to get him some coffee. When she declined and introduced herself, he'd apologized for his oversight, but otherwise he'd busily ignored her. *Just the same, he's my big boss, so I better look busy.* Smallwood strode past her with nary a glance and walked over to Edgar Dunkle, three desks away.

While she had yet to form a strong opinion of Smallwood, her opinion of Dunkle was already set in stone. *The man's a frigging dinosaur!* Past his prime, Dunkle was a slovenly legacy with too much tenure and too many past professional successes to brook much criticism before he retired. Wearing a short-sleeved dress-shirt with wrinkles that suggested several days of wear, he hunched over his messy, paper-strewn, desk, engrossed in a half-eaten sandwich.

The first time Dunkle had seen Mickey's full name on a form, he'd seized on Kitrina Kathleen; sometimes Mickey hated her parents, and he'd promptly dubbed her "KitKat." She'd protested, but the Neanderthal jerk was persistent and soon, to her colossal embarrassment and dismay, it was slowly becoming her office nom-de-guerre.

Smallwood hovered near Dunkle's desk. "Hey Edgar, Gonzales just took a murder call, might be part of that sick ritual serial thing out of Gatesville and Reedley. I want you to drive out to Pickle's Forge and check it out."

Edgar put down his sandwich and looked up. "Pickle's what? Where the hell's that?"

"It's a little nothing town about three hours south and east of Bend; population a little over a thousand."

"Christ Steve," groaned Dunkle, "these bombings are the biggest thing that's happened since the bureau was formed. The whole show's here in Portland."

"I know but someone's gotta look into it and it's your rotation."

"For the love of God! Please Steve, that's fucking hours from here. Can't Pendleton send someone?"

"Ed, we've already loaned them to Salt Lake. There's no one else. This is your baby.

Dunkle scowled and grumbled, "Ok fine, who else gets the short end of the shit-stick?"

"Fraid it's just you Ed," shot back Smallwood. "We're going full-court-press on the bombings and I just can't spare anyone else."

Before Dunkle could respond, Smallwood glanced over and noticed the new gal, *Something or other, Butters,* sitting at a desk fiddling with a cellphone. Except for a couple of blank monitors and a ridiculous Marvel action figure, the desk was completely empty.

"No Ed," instructed Smallwood, "belay that, don't go alone. Take Butters over there."

Mickey, who was eavesdropping, couldn't believe her ears. "Who me?" she blurted, "I only do cyber-crime."

Smallwood immediately turned toward her and looked annoyed. "You've seen the movie 'The Untouchables' right Butters? You've got a gun and a badge don't you?"

"I do," stammered Mickey, "but didn't that guy in the movie get killed?"

"Just say, 'Yes sir'," grunted the agent in charge

Mickey swallowed a couple of times, "Yes sir."

"That's better Agent," growled her boss. "Today is bad enough, don't give me any more grief."

Dunkle looked from his boss to Mickey. "Aw Steve, KitKat, really?"

"That's no grief from either one of you," ordered Smallwood. "It's you two. Now get up and get going!"

As Edgar and Mickey stood up to leave. Smallwood stopped Dunkle and put a hand his arm. "Be careful Ed. Look, I know Butters is not much, but with the rest of us scrambling on the bombings I don't want you hung out there on your own with no backup at all."

Dunkle gave a long-suffering nod and picked up his coat. "Ok Steve, I'll watch it; always do. Come on KitKat." Seething, just short of smoke rolling out of her ears, Mickey trailed Agent Dunkle out of the room and into the elevator.

On the ground floor Edgar led Mickey, still seething, into the parking garage and walked over to the motor pool counter. "Yo, Ernesto, I need to make a run out to Pickle's Forge, some Podunk town that's almost in Idaho. What sort of ride you got for me?"

The pool manager gave Dunkle a sympathetic, long-suffering, look. "I've got a 2010 Crown Vic that's about to be decommissioned."

Edgar turned and stared at an old unmarked CVPI four-door sedan that was sitting off by itself.

"Really, Ernesto? You're kidding, that piece of shit? It's at least seven or more hours to Podunk and that crappy old thing doesn't have cruise control, AC, or even its radio anymore!"

"Sorry Bro! With all the hubbub over the explosions we're tapped out. It is what it is. Take it or leave it."

Edgar scowled at the keys that were pushed toward him across the counter. "God damn it," he grumbled as he scooped them up. "Fine, Ernesto, just remember you fucking owe me big time!" Turning, he glared at Mickey as if the Crown Vic was somehow her fault. "Don't just stand there Butters. Come on."

"Want me to drive?" she asked.

Edgar rolled his eyes. "Jeezus Christ no; just get in!"

Chapter 6

The drive out to Pickle's Forge was proving to be every bit as tedious as Edgar had feared. *Boring, boring, and boring!* The reliable old Crown Vic, on its second tank of gas, rolled down another stretch of empty highway punching its way into the middle of nowhere. Dunkle, still hunkered behind its wheel, rolled his shoulders and tried to work out the knots. Mickey stared out at the dull high-desert scrub and fiddled with her iPhone.

"Another two hours to go," grunted Edgar. "Christ, why couldn't it have been somewhere closer to Portland. Who's ever even heard of Pickle's Forge anyway?"

"I Googled it," enthused Mickey. "It was once a water stop on an unpopular offshoot of the Oregon Trail, founded around 1842. There's not much there today; of course there never was. If you want, I could drive for a while."

"I told you before Butters; I'm the one who does the driving."

"Fine don't get all huffy, I was just offering. I want to help. That's what partners do." Turning back toward her side window, Mickey pulled a second smartphone from her pocket. Holding her iPhone in her right hand and the new phone in her left, she typed quickly with her right thumb.

Edgar looked over bemused. "KitKat, you've been in the office a couple of weeks and your desk is sort of near to mine, but that most emphatically does not make us partners. You're just here to warm that passenger seat until you go back to your cyber stuff, don't screw it up."

"Agent in Charge Smallwood said that I was here to watch your back," snapped Mickey, "and stop calling me KitKat!"

"Well, Steve says a lot of things Butters. When was the last time you were in the field? You're pasty as a maggot from staring at computer screens. I bet you haven't stepped outside since the day you graduated from Quantico."

Suddenly engrossed in her two phones, Mickey seemed deaf. "Hey Ed, I can't find the Internet."

"Really? Oh my gawd; that is just terrible! Are you sure?"

"Yeah," answered Mickey oblivious to the sarcasm. "I lost signal on my iPhone maybe three miles back. My other cell can't find a signal either and they each use different service providers. Wow, this is creepy!"

Dunkle kept his hands glued to the steering wheel, but turned his head to stare.

"So Butters, you got a boyfriend or a girlfriend? I certainly hope so, because you really, really need to get a life."

"Okay Boomer," glared Mickey, "anything you say!"

Two hours later, with her iPhone finally displaying one bar, but still without Internet, the Crown Vic rolled into Pickle's Forge. "Thank God, at last!" sighed Edgar.

The town was small enough, that if he had ignored its posted 20 mph speed limit and blinked twice, they might have missed it. Except for a couple of parked cars, its main drag was empty. Dunkle slowed to a crawl and examined the town. The homes and few businesses that lined the street had seen better days, but just the same the place looked neat and well kept.

"Hey, Ed," suggested Mickey, "that place across the street looks promising." In response, Dunkle made a wide U-turn and guided the Crown Vic to the curb in front of a tidy brick building with a tiny lawn out front. The grass was green and neatly trimmed. In the middle of the patch an antique sign identified the building as the Pickle's Forge "City Hall."

"Okay," said Dunkle opening his door. "This should be the place, time to put on our game faces."

Game faces? thought Mickey. *You gotta be kidding.* No sooner had the two of them closed their doors and discretely stretched than a tall good-looking young man walked out of the building. Instantly spotting them, he descended the four concrete steps and headed straight their way. Like a character out of a classic western, he was dressed in a khaki shirt with a military cut, Levis, cowboy boots and a cowboy hat. A conspicuous star-shaped badge decorated his shirt and on his hip rested a huge six-shooter in western holster.

"Howdy, you two the FBI?" he grinned.

"Yes sir," replied Ed. "I'm Special Agent Edgar Dunkle and this is my partner, Special Agent Kitrina Butters." *Will wonders never cease?* thought Mickey slightly taken aback.

The young cop eagerly extended his hand. "Mighty glad to see you folks; I'm the chief of police, Walter Teague. All my friends call me Buzz. Man, am I ever glad that you're here. What with those terrorists and all, we were worried that no one would show."

You're right Chief," soothed Mickey. "Things are a little crazy out there, but crime doesn't sleep. We're sorry it took us so long."

"Like I said, I'm just real glad that you're here," admitted Teague. "This murder's by far the worst thing that's ever happened in Pickle's Forge. We don't have experience with stuff like this. Hell, most folks around here don't even lock their doors."

"Excuse me for asking chief," broke in Dunkle, "but isn't your town a little small and a little off the beaten track to have its own police force?"

Buzz glanced sheepishly at the older FBI agent's attractive FBI partner. "Well yeah. Tell the truth, it's a volunteer position. Me and Leroy, that's my deputy Leroy Caderette, we just sorta help out. We catch a few speeders in the summer and sometimes the boys over at the Elks get a little rowdy."

"Speeders huh?" mused Dunkle.

"Yeah a few, the mayor gives me a budget and lets me use an office here in city hall. Leroy and I also check the parking meters. It's all just part-time for now. Of course, someday, I plan to run for County Sheriff. Mickey looked left and right down the street. Only four parking meters were in sight.

"Okay Chief, fair enough," nodded Dunkle. "I guess you better tell us about your murder."

"Well, I expect you otta see the crime scene first. Leroy n' I left it just like Andy Cates found it. Didn't touch nothing, just taped it off."

Edgar threw Mickey a look, "I'm sure you did just fine, Chief."

"Alright then," said Buzz. "Why don't I grab my truck and you can follow me out. I'll fill you in on everything we know once we get there."

"Lead on Chief," replied Mickey. "Special Agent Dunkle and I are right behind you."

Buzz pulled some keys from his pocket and walked toward a pickup parked on the street. Magnetic signs stuck to the truck's doors proclaimed, "Pickle's Forge Police, Protect and Serve." As soon as Teague's back was turned and he'd gotten a few paces away, Edgar turned and gave Mickey a soft cuff to the back of her head.

"Jesus Christ, Butters, 'Crime doesn't sleep!' What the Hell is wrong with you? You're not Joe Friday. This isn't friggin Dragnet. Try to remember it!

Chapter 7

A mile or two out of town, Teague turned left onto a one-lane blacktop that zigzagged back and forth along what Mickey assumed were property boundaries. After another mile or so, he swung right onto a dirt track running through the middle of tall stands of corn. Bumping along behind him Dunkle had begun to wonder about the Crown Vic's ground clearance when the young chief pulled over into an area of flattened stalks and parked beside two other cars. Hopping out, he waved for Dunkle and Butters to pull in behind him. Once they were also out of their car, he smiled and beckoned.

"Over this way," he gestured. The body's about fifty yards in. I know you're both pros, but I still think I better warn you; it's pretty ugly. I've seen a lot of livestock butchered; but I've never seen nothing even close to this."

"Thanks Buzz. We appreciate the heads-up," reassured Dunkle, "but we'll be okay. Lead the way."

Teague headed briskly into the corn with Dunkle tight on his heels. After pausing for a moment,

Mickey followed several paces behind them looking decidedly apprehensive. Walking along what had by now become a beaten path, they soon stepped out from among tall green stalks and out into the open.

Mickey took one look, almost swooned, and averted her eyes. The crows were gone, but the body was still nailed to the ground. Someone had trampled more corn at the edge of the opening to enlarge it and wooden stakes had been driven around its border to support a perimeter of crime tape. Trying to avoid the body, she stared at the two men who were waiting just outside the tape. One was lanky with oily hair, dressed in a cheap business suit with his jacket thrown over one shoulder. A cigarette dangled carelessly from his mouth and his right hand clutched a fancy looking camera. The other fellow was overweight and munching on a half-eaten maple bar. His baggy jeans looked like they needed a wash and his blue work-shirt hung untucked over his belly. A black baseball cap on his head proclaimed, "Police," and, just like Chief Teague, he sported a shiny silver star pinned on his chest.

"Jeez Buzz," reproached the guy with the maple bar, "it's about time. Me 'n Corky are going to have the creeps for months."

"I'm sorry guys," answered Teague. "It took the Feds a long time to get here. This rough looking character is Special Agent Dunkle and his good-looking partner here is Special Agent Butters." Dizzier by the minute, Mickey didn't know whether to feel insulted or flattered by Teague's sexist comment. She didn't abide chauvinists, but still it wasn't that often that a handsome young man complimented her looks.

The heavyset fellow moved closer, wiped greasy maple bar crumbs on his pant leg and held out his ostensibly clean hand. "Pleased to meet you. I'm Buzz's deputy, Leroy Caderette. This scrawny feller over here with the camera is Corky Jones, Pickle Forge's own representative of the Fourth Estate."

Jones also stepped forward. "Owner and editor of the Weekly Forge Tribune at your service, awfully glad that you're here."

Mickey and Edgar each dutifully shook the two proffered hands. "Deputy, Mister Jones," muttered Dunkle.

"Over there," offered Caderette, "that's what's left of poor Jane Carhill. Janie wasn't our most upstanding citizen, but she wasn't a bad gal and nobody deserves that." The deputy's words again drew everyone attention to the body. The only thing that Mickey saw was all the blood. The spinning in her head got worse and she could feel herself turn green and begin to sweat. *Please God no*, she thought.

"Nailed her to the damn ground and then chopped her head clean off!" blurted Jones.

"What kind of sick animal does something like this?" sighed Teague.

Blood, blood everywhere, so much blood! Suddenly insubstantial, the earth seemed to move under Mickey's feet. Her legs turned to jelly. Detached, she watched herself in slow motion as she slowly spiraled into the crime tape and then sprawled face down onto the trampled corn stalks.

"Good Lord," uttered Corky Jones, the first to rush over. "Agent Butters, are you alright?"

"I'm okay," she muttered, still lying on the ground.

As everyone crowded around, Edgar dropped to a knee beside her, tucked an arm under her shoulder, and gently lifted her into a sitting position. "Are you sure Kitrina?" he asked with genuine concern. "What happened?"

More wonders, she thought. "Really Edgar, I'm okay, just overheated I guess."

"Yeah," volunteered Caderette, "lot of that going around, Buzz here puked himself when he first saw her."

"It's not that, I'm just too hot!" countered Mickey sounding more peevish than she intended.

Dunkle climbed back to his feet. "Okay Butters, you sit there and cool off," he advised, now sounding a bit patronizing. "I'll get everybody's statements and show Mister Jones here how to photograph a crime scene."

Keeping her eyes carefully averted from the late Jane Carhill, Mickey slowly stood and moved carefully to a shadier spot at the edge of the corn. As she began to sit back down, Buzz Teague gently reached out and took her arm. "Here, let me help you." A shy smile lit his face. For the next hour she watched as Dunkle took notes in an old-school memo pad and Jones snapped pictures. Because of the long drive from Portland, it was already late in the day and, by the time he stopped, the newspaperman was using his flash.

"Okay, I think we're done here," announced Dunkle. "That's about all we can do for now. Anything more's going to have to wait for the lab boys."

By that time Mickey, although still averting her eyes, was back on her feet and much recovered. "Hey Ed," she called. I know the scene's pretty disturbed, but do you think we should put up some more crime tape?"

For a moment Edgar gave her a look that said he'd forgotten that she was still there. "Yeah Butters, you do that," he agreed, then he turned to Teague. "So Buzz, when we leave here can you round up someone to sit out on the road and shoo off any thrill seekers?

"Sure, no problem, Agent Dunkle, but what do we do about poor Janie? We can't just leave her out here."

"No, of course not, where's the county coroner's office?"

"That's over in Bend, but it takes nearly three hours to make the drive and every time I called their line reported 'temporarily out of service.'"

"Okay, forget the coroner," replied Dunkle, "just call a mortuary."

"Ain't got one of those," drawled Caderette

"That's Bend too," added Jones

"How about an ambulance?" sighed Dunkle

"Ain't got one of those neither."

"So then, what do you have?" scowled the special agent, quickly growing exasperated.

"Well, I've got some black plastic sheeting in my pickup," proposed Buzz. "I suppose we could wrap her up in that and then put her in the back."

"Guess it'll have to do Chief, better go grab it." As Teague disappeared into the corn, Dunkle and Butters exchanged a look.

Chapter 8

Except for the Elks Club and the Sidle Inn, Pickle's Forge rolled up its streets the moment it got dark. Local institution Green's Market had accordingly buttoned up for the night and a large "CLOSED" sign hung visibly inside its padlocked front door. Barely illuminated by a streetlight down the block, Mickey stood on the market's ramshackle covered-porch and watched Edgar and Deputy Caderette.

A few steps away hunkered a large metal vending box that was labeled, "ICE." It was also decorated with a pair of smiling penguins outfitted in mufflers and cute wool caps. The doors of the box stood open, and the two men were wrestling a plastic wrapped body through the opening. Buzz Teague and Carol Green, the market's glowering owner, stood off to the side.

"God damn it Buzz! You shouldn't have called me! I don't like this. I don't like it one bit! You got no right to put her in there. What happens to my ice business if someone finds out?"

"Christ almighty Carol," pleaded Buzz. "We already went through this. There's nowhere else, and no one's going to find out!"

"How do you know they won't? You tell me that! You reach in there for a bag of ice and I think it's going to be pretty god damn obvious!"

"That's not going to happen," assured Edgar, as Caderette slammed the ice box shut with a sepulchral *thunk*. "We're going to throw on a heavy padlock. Everything will be fine."

"Great, that's just great," grumbled Carol. "And, what if someone wants some ice?"

"Put up an 'Out of Order' sign," suggested Mickey. "Anyone asks, just tell 'em it's broken."

"Well, what about my ice?" demanded Carol. "Word's gonna get out and no one's gonna want it after this. Who's gonna pay for my ice?"

"Good God Carol! Jane's dead," groaned Buzz. "Just bill me!"

Mrs. Green stalked off still grumbling and only slightly mollified. After she pulled out in her old gold Galaxy 500, pealing rubber to show her displeasure with Pickle's Forge's finest, Caderette snapped their padlock onto the icebox.

"I feel bad about this," said Buzz, "but until we can get the coroner out here, I think this is the best we can do."

"Alright Chief, try not to worry about it," calmed Dunkle. "You're improvising in a tough situation and you're doing well." At his words, Buzz seemed to stand a little taller. "Now," continued Dunkle, "lets head over your office at city hall and take a good hard look at what we're dealing with."

As Dunkle and Butters walked back to their Crown Vic, Mickey turned around for another look at the humming ice box sitting on the darkened porch. "Do you really think this is going to be okay?"

Edgar also paused and looked back. "It's pretty messed up, but as long as the power doesn't go out I think we're good."

Back at City Hall, Buzz unlocked the front door and they all trooped inside. The "Police Department" proved to be a small windowless room at the back. Buzz led the way and plopped down behind an old oak desk. Except for a dinosaur-age rotary phone, a pencil holder, and a plastic plaque that read "Walter Teague – Chief of Police," the desk's surface was empty. Mickey looked around. To call the space Spartan was a gross understatement. Someone had thumbtacked a county map and a few wanted posters onto the walls. Leroy Caderette had wedged himself in next to a tin four-drawer file cabinet leaving two folding chairs in front of the desk for the FBI agents. A mostly empty gun rack that held a cheap security shotgun and an open box of shells rounded out the office décor.

Buzz leaned forward and waved Edgar and Mickey into the folding chairs. "Let's leave the door open. No one else is in the building at this hour and it gets hot as hades in here if you close it. So, Agent Dunkle, what-da-ya think? What's our next step?"

"Without forensics we can't be certain, Chief, but from what we saw in the cornfield Agent Butters and I are maybe ninety percent sure we know your purp."

"If it's who we think it is," elaborated Mickey, "the FBI has tracked the bastard for a really long time. We know a lot about his MO."

"That's the good news," threw-in Edgar. "The bad news is that, if we're right about who it is, the guy is one sick and twisted puppy."

Mickey continued, "You saw how Miss Carhill's body was arranged like a perverted parody of the crucifixion. The FBI's psych profile says the murderer is most likely some kind of fixated religious nut."

"We think he may have killed fifteen women so far," explained Edgar. "Sixteen if you count Miss Carhill. Four turned up dead in Gatesville, Texas two years back and then another three last year in Reedley, Idaho. Those were the worst. The others were single murders, spread around and separated by time and distance."

"Oh Wow! No shit?" exclaimed Leroy, shifting his position against the file-cabinet. "I don't remember hearing nothing creepy like that. Sometimes Ol' Corky misses a story or two and doesn't get 'em into his Weekly Tribune, but that shoulda been real sensational news."

"It was touch and go," responded Edgar, "but the bureau worked hard to suppress it. When it wants to throw its weight around, the FBI's has a lot of clout."

"Your Jane Carhill's just like the others," added Mickey. "Every one of them was staked out, stabbed through the side, and decapitated. No sexual assault. The weirdest part is that all their injuries were inflicted post-mortem."

Chief Teague looked confused. "What do you mean, post-mortem?"

Dunkle shook his head. "Just that, Buzz. The coroners' reports all say that the victims were already dead well before he nailed 'em down and cut their heads off.

"Sweet Jesus!" sputtered Caderette.

"Leroy, you think that's weird," confided Dunkle, "nobody knows definitively what killed 'em. The techies diced and sliced and ran every damn test in the book, but the only thing we know for sure is that the women were already dead."

"Okay, where does that leave us? What do we do now?" asked Buzz

"I told you that we know the guy's MO," answered Mickey, "but unfortunately we don't actually know much about him. They found a partial footprint in Reedley so the bureau thinks he's about six-foot 200 pounds, that's about it."

"If we can get through, Agent Butters and I will call in and explain the situation here in Pickle's Forge to our agent in charge," said Dunkle. "Frankly I doubt it'll do much good. With nearly 6,000 bomb casualties in five West Coast cities the chances of us getting any sort of backup out here are pretty much zilch. For now, it's just us."

"The thing is," added Mickey looking uncomfortable, "if we don't stop this guy, and he sticks to his previous MO, we're probably looking at more dead."

"Like I said," repeated Buzz, "what do we do now? You're the FBI; what can the four of us do? What's our next step?"

To the others' surprise, Leroy straightened up from his slouch against the cabinet and the wall. "Ya know, Bobby Earl said he saw Jane leave the Sidle Inn last night at a little after midnight along with Mary Beth Barger. Maybe we could start with that?"

Chapter 9

By a long shot, The States Motel's best assets were its prices. When the national average for a motel room was running $420 and the average for a Motel 6 was $78.86, The States was a true outlier at $25, or in Gideon's case $30 per night plus tip. Just because it was cheap, didn't mean the old place was a bargain. In Pickle's Forge you got what you paid for. Room number eight was gloomy, disquieting, and poorly maintained. Gideon didn't care. He knelt in the dark, in the the middle of the stained wall-to-wall carpet, and hung his head in prayer. A rough homemade-looking iron cross lay on the floor in front of him and an equally crude homemade flail lay by his right hand. Gideon's back was covered with welts and scars, some old, a few still fresh.

"I try Lord," he moaned quietly. "Really I do, but my flesh is so weak, so weak. He waits. He's everywhere. He taunts me. He tempts me. He calls to me day and night, and, oh God forgive me, I listen. I can't shut him out. I want to. I try, but I can't. Give me the power to resist your enemy Lord; the will to do thy work. Help this frail mortal to mete out your vengeance. Lend strength to my arm. Amen."

When Gideon finished his prayer, he put on his cleanest shirt, fit his clip-on tie, and buttoned his MBTA conductor's jacket. Walking over to the bed, he picked up his small nondescript duffle bag. Next, he stepped over to a table that was bolted to the wall. His fancy pool cue case sat on the table. Next to the case lay a wooden mallet and a number of large iron nails of the kind you might use to secure a tent. The contents of the case was his most prized possession. He undid its brass latches with reverence and carefully opened the lid. The object inside was a thing of beauty. Nestled in the case's thick velvet lining lay a long, wide, iron spearhead. The body of the blade was thin and its edges were honed to razor sharpness. Although the weapon was hundreds of years old, it was carefully oiled and not a hint of rust marred its surface. Along with the blade, the case contained a polished hardwood shaft that Gideon deftly fitted into the spear point's shank. He'd first seen the assegai in a glass display case in a small rural museum. Made by some long-dead southern

African people, God had told him that, just as he was the Lord's instrument, the spear was to be his. He'd returned after dark broken the glass case and stolen it.

Scooping the mallet and spikes into his duffle and hefting the spear, Gideon crossed the miserable little room and opened its door. Before stepping into the darkness outside, he waited and looked warily about. No one was visible, so he hurried silently away, leaving The States Motel with long distance eating strides.

At the town hall, the two FBI agents and Pickle's Forge's "police force" still huddled around Buzz Teague's desk. "I don't know what a couple of eighteen-year-old girls were doing at the Sidle Inn after Midnight, but I intend to find out," declared Buzz.

"What-da-ya say we drive out and talk to Luther?" suggested Caderette. "You know that grizzly old bastard is sure to be there until he closes."

"I've warned Luther before," grumbled Buzz. "If he's serving underage again, we're going to do a lot more than just talk!"

Everyone jumped a bit when the old-style rotary phone on Teague's desk began to ring. Buzz looked at his watch and picked it up. "Pickle's Forge Police, Chief Teague speaking. Yes, that's right. Thanks for returning my call." Holding his hand over the mouthpiece, he whispered to the others, "It's Mrs. Barger down on Chapel Lane." Then, removing his hand, he resumed talking. "How long? Ok, are you sure? Anywhere you can think of she might be? No, don't worry. I'm certain she's fine. We're just checking into some underage drinking. Yep, yep, we'll find her and bring her on home. Ok thanks." Hanging up the phone, he stared at the others. "I don't like the sound of that. She says that she can't find Mary Beth and hasn't seen her in two days.

"Mary Beth's pretty wild," claimed Caderette, "but two days is unusual. Thing is she's real tight with Jane. The two of 'em do everything... did everything together."

"Could be she's in trouble," admitted Mickey, "but maybe she just saw something and got scared or maybe she's just off somewhere with some boy."

"Let's run down to Ray's junkyard, proposed Leroy. There's an old trailer out there that some of the rougher kids use as a clubhouse."

"It's supposed to be a secret," threw in Buzz, "but if they don't cause any trouble, we don't let on that we know."

"If she's scared or just out heavy petting with a boyfriend and doesn't want her mamma to know, it's a place she might go," said Leroy

"So what's it going to be, Chief," asked Dunkle, "the Sidle Inn or the junkyard?

"With Mary Beth missing," reasoned Buzz, "I think it ought to be the junkyard."

On leaving the city hall, Dunkle suggested that the four of them ride together in the Crown Vic. When the others agreed, he assumed his regular position behind the wheel. Mickey and Leroy climbed in the backseat, and Buzz took shotgun so that he could navigate. After a minute or two of driving in the town's outskirts, he gestured ahead.

"Okay, slow down now. See there, coming up on the left, turn there."

The Vic's headlights swept off the pavement onto an oiled dirt road, momentarily throwing their beams across a large weathered sign, "Ray's Auto Wrecking and Scrap Metal, No Trespassing." Some wag with a large marking pen had scrawled "Crazy" above the word, "Ray's."

"It's just over this rise, maybe two hundred yards," continued Buzz. When the Vic crested the hummock and the darkened junkyard, surrounded by a dilapidated corrugated metal fence, suddenly popped into view, Dunkle put on the brakes.

"Whoa, this place is huge!" he exclaimed. "I wouldn't have expected a salvage yard this size in a town as small as Pickle's Forge."

"It's been here for two generations," explained Leroy from the back seat. "Anything around here that breaks down, this is where it usually ends up. Even a lot of cars whose owners believed they were just passing through are rusting away in there. When I was a kid, Ray's old man, Ray senior, ran the place as a true business. You know, taking stuff in, selling parts and scrap back out, with guard dogs, and all. Not our boy Ray, he's cracked as a shithouse rat. He just keeps adding stuff."

"Will he be around to unlock things and corral the dogs," asked Mickey

"Naw," returned Leroy, "That was back in Ray senior's day. The dogs are long gone and the gate fell off its hinges years ago. The only time Ray junior comes around is when he's adding more treasure to his hoard."

"Alright then," said Dunkle as he guided the Vic through the one-time gate, "let's check it out."

Inside the ramshackle fence, everything was pitch black. The car's headlights picked out a tumbledown building with "Office" painted in faded letters on its door. Edgar pulled the car to a stop and shut off the engine. When he turned off the Vic's headlights the darkness grew even deeper. As everyone climbed out and into a feeble pool of moonlight, he looked over at Buzz.

"You and Leroy said kids have a hangout in here, Chief. Where is it?"

"Way out over there," said Buzz, pointing. "It's an old semi-trailer that's missing its axles, almost at the back fence. We have to walk from here. Ray doesn't care if anything ever leaves so there's no driveways anymore, just winding paths through the junk."

"Chief, you point the way," instructed Dunkle in his best authoritative FBI voice. "When we get there, you and Leroy hang back. Special Agent Butters and I are the professionals here and we'll take the lead."

"With all due respect, Agent Dunkle, screw that," snapped Buzz. "Leroy and I might not get paid for what we do but this is our town and our people. There's no way we're going to just sit in the car."

"Hold on there, don't get your nose out of joint," placated Edgar. "No one's telling you two to sit in the car. Just let Agent Butters and I take the lead when we get close."

"Okay, well sure, just so you remember that we're a part of this too."

"We're glad that you're here," added Mickey.

"You'll be right behind us," reassured Edgar. "It's like the bottom of a well out here, help me get flashlights out of the trunk." As they walked around the car, Buzz nudged Leroy and gave him a satisfied look.

Chapter 10

The demon was close, very close. Its pull had grown strong and unrelenting. It had guided Gideon through small darkened streets and cluttered back alleys, around the edge of the town, and out into an open field of withered grass and scrub. That's where he spotted the woman. Her feet were bare and she was dressed in a yellow halter-top and skin-tight jeans. From a single glimpse, he knew that he was too late. *The demon has taken her,* sighed Gideon as though in pain. *Why Lord? You are stronger than the evil one. Why do you allow him his perversions? Why do you again give me this burden of your cross to bear? Though I question your will, still, I am your obedient servant.* In his heart, Gideon knew that the woman was no longer a woman. She was no longer an innocent. *True death can be her only release.*

His sigh must have carried into the stillness of the night. The young woman turned toward him. To Gideon her face seemed to glow unnaturally white in the moonlight. They stared at one another for perhaps a single heartbeat, then she exploded into startled movement and began to run. She ran hard. She ran as though her life depended on it. She had a head start of perhaps seventy yards. Gideon couldn't allow her to escape, so he ran harder. His legs were longer than hers, and each gasping stride closed a bit of the distance between them. As they ran, a rickety wall of corrugated metal grew out of the darkness. *Nowhere to go now!* exulted Gideon. As fast as his thought, the woman twisted her body in an unnatural fashion and plunged through a sudden hole in in the corroded barrier.

Gideon reached the ragged hole and stooped down to cautiously follow. *She's one of his,* he thought. *I must be wary of deceit. I mustn't let down my guard.* Inside the wall, he found himself inside a sprawling maze of wrecked vehicles, discarded appliances, and rusting debris of every conceivable description. Except for a rime of moonlight that rendered the scene foreign and dreamlike, darkness ruled in every direction. The pull told him that she was hidden somewhere just steps away. He waited silently, coiled and tense. A slight flicker of movement grabbed at the corner of his eye.

The fiend's minion tried to flee, it burst from one hiding place, straining to reach another. Gideon reacted on instinct. She feinted left and then to the right, but he countered and forced her back. Cornered, she whirled to face him. Her hands extended toward him, fists clenched. Her face displayed a feral mask of existential fear and rage. With her lips drawn back from her teeth, she snarled and screamed. In the red flash of her eyes Gideon gazed into the burning depths of Hell.

Lord guide my hand, he prayed as, seeking her heart, he drove his spear into Mary Beth Barger's side. Eyes startled and wide, she stared into his soul and continued to shriek. "It's almost over," he soothed. Her screaming guttered and he lowered her gently to the ground. "There, isn't that better?" He smoothed her hair. She was almost free of the demon's hold. The iron had pierced her heart and only one duty remained. Gideon shook the stakes and mallet out of his bag.

Moving warily between towering piles of junk, Mickey gasped and everyone froze in their tracks as the first terrifying screech shattered the stillness. The eerie screams continued and Dunkle pulled out his short service revolver.

"Holy Mary!" whispered Mickey. "What was that?"

"Not sure," answered Buzz. It sounds like a mountain lion screaming." Then, as suddenly as they had begun, the unnerving shrieks abruptly ended.

"I may be a city boy," declared Dunkle, "but that was no damn cat! Where'd those screams come from?"

"Off to our right, over that way," pointed Leroy.

"Come on," urged Buzz drawing his big Colt Peacemaker. "Let's go!" Dunkle nodded his assent and Mickey and Leroy also drew their weapons. With many guarded looks, the four of them began to edge stealthily in the direction of the sound.

Out of sight, but not far ahead, Gideon hurried to finish his God's work. He'd arranged the thing that used to be Mary Beth Barger into the form of the Lord's cross and pounded stakes into her left hand and into her feet. On his knees, he stretched out her other hand. *I hate this!* he thought. Sweat beaded his forehead. His face felt hot and feverish but, as he raised his mallet to drive the last spike, a chill draft prickled the hairs on the back of his neck. Twisting, he stared into the dark. Glowing animal eyes stared back.

"I knew you were there," croaked Gideon. "I felt you watching." As he remained motionless, the demon stepped out from the shadows. Exactly like every other time that he'd ever appeared, he was tall, blond, and impeccably dressed. Not a speck of dust or an out of place hair marred his unnaturally handsome appearance.

"Gideon, Gideon, Gideon," he chuckled, "what am I ever going to do with you? You keep stealing and breaking my toys. I'm starting to get a little annoyed."

"Why do you do that?" complained Gideon.

"Why do you do that?"

"Why do you talk in my voice?"

"Why do you talk in my voice?" echoed the demon.

"Stop it!" demanded Gideon.

"Stop it!"

The evil one edged closer. Gideon leapt to his feet, snatched up his spear and brandished it in front of him. "Keep back fiend!" he hissed. "In the name of the Lord I order you, be gone!" The monster bent at his waist and giggled holding his belly.

"Really Gideon, after all this time, everything we've shared, I thought you'd know better. Put down that ridiculous spear. The girl is mine!"

"Too late," glared Gideon. "This child is nearly free. When your evil's left her, I'm coming for you! I've defeated those you've cursed. You're next!"

The demon threw back his head howled with laughter. "Ah Robinson, you may not have any sense of humor, but you never cease to entertain me." In response, Gideon turned back toward Mary Beth and raised his spear above his head, holding it in both hands like an ax.

"Gideon," shrilled the demon, "I'm warning you leave my plaything alone!" A cloud shifted and Gideon stood exposed in a pool of moonlight.

At the same instant, Special Agent Dunkle, slightly ahead, led his little group around a corner in the twisting labyrinth of junk. Twenty yards away, his eyes met with a frozen tableau, a figment plucked from nightmares. A woman lay on the ground and a lone man stood next to her. His back was toward Dunkle, but high above him glistened a long dripping blade.

"Hold right there!" roared Dunkle

"FBI!" yelled Mickey, who was right on his heels.

Ignoring their frantic shouts, the man hunched his powerful shoulders and swung the blade. Mickey shuddered at the hollow sound as it struck the woman. Then, the head rolled free. *Oh Dear God!* she thought, *The blood. There'll be blood everywhere!*

"Son of a bitch!" screamed Teague; then both he and Dunkle dashed forward, firing their pistols. Bright muzzle flashes lit the junkyard like flashes of lightning, illuminating and blinding at the same time. The man hesitated over his kill for the briefest of moments, then he plunged headlong into the deeper darkness of the junkyard.

"Did we, did we hit him?" stuttered Buzz. "I thought I saw him stagger."

"Hell if I know," threw back Dunkle, "but I'm not letting that evil bastard get away! Come on, Chief!" Flashlights seeking ahead, the two men charged off in pursuit.

"Holy shit!" gasped Leroy. "That was; I've never seen anything like that!"

Blood! thought Mickey as the two of them, now alone, walked toward the decapitated body. *I should be with Edgar. I'm supposed to back him up. Blood!* She glanced at the gory corpse and her vision narrowed and her stomach churned. *How can Leroy lean so close? Blood everywhere!*

"Oh Christ! Damn! Agent Butters, it's her alright. It's Mary Beth, and just like poor Janie." Mickey's eyes rolled back. The next thing she knew, she was on the ground and Caderette was kneeling beside her, gently slapping her cheeks. "Wake up Agent Butters! What's wrong? Are you hurt?"

Feeling weak, slightly disorientated, and thoroughly embarrassed, she pushed him away and sat up. "No I'm ok, I just sort of fainted." Leroy stared at her with a confused and slightly hurt expression. "I'm sorry," she gushed. "Look, I can't help it all right. I'm hemophobic."

"Well I don't think we've got any gays here in Pickle's Forge. Maybe Gene and Alvin that own the antique store, but I don't see what that's got to do with anything right now."

"Jesus Christ, Leroy, not homophobic, hemophobic; I get physically ill at the sight of blood."

Leroy stared at her. "Wow; that must be kind of tough considering your choice of career, Agent Butters."

Mickey looked back, shamefaced. "I lied on my FBI application. My area of expertise is cybercrime. I mostly work in the office. The spells pass pretty quickly. I never thought it would come up."

"Crap Mickey," sighed Leroy. "You mean you're not really an FBI agent?

"No, I'm a real agent it's just that..." Gunfire and shouting echoed from deeper inside the junkyard and swallowed anything else that she was about to say.

Near a darker passage in the scrapheap's northwest corner, Dunkle and Teague paused. Both men breathed heavily. "I think maybe you did wing him," mouthed Buzz. "I think he's dragging a foot."

"If he's gone to ground," answered Dunkle pointing, "in there, in that tangle, is going to be where he's hiding. I'll tail him in. You hot foot around behind, then I'll drive him toward you. Be careful, I don't want that big cannon of yours taking my head off."

"Alright, but you watch it too," replied Teague as he gripped his Colt and sprinted off to the right.

Dunkle watched Buzz disappear into the shadows and then he edged forward into a narrow gap in the junk. Holding his service piece out in front of him he slipped through the towering piles of rusted scrap. He was a heavy man, but he moved with a stealth that belied his size. As one tense minute after another stretched by, Edgar began to weigh the likelihood that the killer had somehow managed to elude him. Creeping around a discarded commercial refrigerator, he stepped into a small open space. With his flashlight clicked off, he squinted into the deeper darkness ahead. The moonlight was dim, but it was just bright enough that he noticed an even darker shadow fall across his back.

Teague was still running hard when he heard Edgar's shout. "FBI! FBI!" His chest pounding, he skidded to a stop as the night's oppressive stillness shattered with the sound of gunfire. Again and again, he heard the distant reports of Dunkle's service revolver, then silence, then nothing.

Buzz shouted into the darkness. "Dunkle? Agent Dunkle are you all right? Can you hear me? Agent Dunkle!" Not even tiny night sounds answered him back. Worried and apprehensive, holding his own gun tightly with both hands, Buzz moved slowly toward a dark opening that beckoned amid the junk. *This has to be the end of the tunnel Edgar entered.* He paused at the edge of the dark passage and strained his ears.

After what felt almost an eternity, he heard something, a soft metallic tapping sound. Screwing up his courage and taking a tighter grip on his pistol, Teague flicked off his flashlight and stole silently forward into the passage. With each cautious step the odd sound grew louder.

Whatever it is, it's got to be right here. Switching his light back on, he found himself staring down at an old dented Studebaker hubcap lying only inches in front of his feet. Something dripped into it. "Tap. Tap. Tap." Leaning over, Buzz touched his index finger to the dark liquid. It felt warm. Illuminated in the glare of his flashlight, he knew in an instant that it was blood. Jerking back, suddenly sickened, he aimed his flashlight above him.

He's dead! How can he be anything else? screamed the voice in Teague's head. The jagged piece of exhaust pipe that held Edgar in place jutted from his savaged chest. The blood ran slowly down its length and dribbled into space.

"Oh God! Leroy, Leroy, Agent Butters!" screamed Buzz. "For Christ's sake, he's killed Dunkle! Get over here!"

Almost out of earshot, Mickey and Caderette still stood hesitating near Mary Beth Barger's decapitated remains. Shaky and sweating, it was all Mickey could do to pretend that it wasn't there. "Do you think the killer was alone? I swear I heard him talking to someone."

"I didn't see anybody else," answered Caderette, "but, after Buzz and Ed run off, I thought I heard shooting, maybe a lot of shooting."

"I'll admit I'm pretty out of it," responded Mickey. "I'm not sure that I heard anything. I don't trust myself much right now. There, what's that?"

"Someone's shouting. I think it's Buzz!" Almost before the words left Leroy's mouth, the shouting was followed by a flurry of far-off gunfire. "I know that sound! That's Buzz's big old Colt," gushed Leroy. "Shit, what do you think we should do?"

Mickey, considered for a moment, while a strange look played across her face. "I don't know about you, but I'm going back to the car for the shotgun." Without another word, she turned away from the headless corpse and began to jog back toward the Crown Vic.

Leroy cast a couple of quick anxious looks into the darkness and then hurried after her. "Hey Mickey, wait up!"

Not that far away as the crow flies, next to a dented hubcap filled with fresh blood, a pair of vise-like hands, as strong and as unyielding as steel, gave Buzz Teague's head a sudden sharp twist. Accompanied by the sound of cracking bones his neck assumed an anatomically impossible angle. Released, he staggered once, then sprawled violently onto a patch of oily dirt. His body twitched a couple of times because it didn't understand that it was already dead; then, it lay still. The young chief's eyes, permanently fixed, wide with offended surprise, appeared to stare upward into a stygian void.

When Mickey's younger self had daydreamed about her life as an FBI agent, she'd envisioned herself outwitting evil cyber criminals and foiling foreign black-hat hackers as they attempted to use bits and bytes to scuttle the American way. She'd never considered, not even for a single second, an old ice vending machine in Pickle's Forge, Oregon stuffed with four bodies wrapped in crinkly black plastic. Before Leroy had closed the door and replaced the padlock, she'd stared into that dark cramped space. Amid Mrs. Green's bags of ice, a slight unsettling mist of warmth rose from two of the bundles.

Helping transport Edgar and Buzz from the awfulness of the junkyard to the ghastliness of Green's Market, was far and away the worst thing Mickey had ever endured. Walking back through it in her head, she seriously doubted that she could have managed if it had been just her and Caderette. On reaching the Vic, she'd tried to call her regional office for backup. Every one of her frantic attempts had finished in utter futility, thwarted by an endlessly repeating, "All-circuits-are-busy," message. Leroy's own panicky phone calls had yielded better results.

After an endless eighteen minute wait, a heavy-duty dually pickup truck had roared through the junkyard entrance and skidded to a stop next to the

Vic. When its doors popped open Corky Jones, the newspaper owner, and two other men had jumped out, all of them holding guns. The truck's driver had introduced himself to Mickey as Councilman Bud Fellers. The other man turned out to be Crazy Ray, the scrapyard's owner.

Surprisingly, Ray's junkyard proved to be wired with a veritable rat's nest of string lights. As soon as he switched them on, "So's I can make sure nothing ain't missing!" the piles of junk glowed like an upscale mall on a Saturday night. With the unexpected light, the danger and shadows seemed to slowly melt away. Left behind were three brightly lit scenes of horror, and hours of grisly responsibility.

Chapter 11

Although it was nearly dawn, darkness continued to hold sway and electric light poured from the windows of Pickle's Forge city hall. In Buzz Teague's office empty coffee cups and two full ash trays littered his once clean desk. Jean Rudolph, the town's three-term mayor, sat behind the desk in the dead chief's chair. Leaning back, she looked at the other four people crowded into the small room: the young FBI special agent, Kitrina Butters, dumpy Leroy Caderette, bespectacled Corky Jones, and gruff Bud Fellers. They all looked tired, frazzled, and worse for wear.

Jean carefully knocked a long ash from her cigarette. "Christ, Buzz is really dead; I just can't get my head around it. I knew that reckless boy since he was in diapers. Hell, I went to high school with his momma! I shoulda never let him put on that stupid badge. Dammit I shouldn't have let him talk me into it!"

"Don't beat yourself up Jean," urged Fellers. "You couldn't have known it would lead to this.

Nobody could have. It was just 'cops and robbers' none of us took him seriously."

"I did!" blurted Leroy.

"Yeah, well nobody takes you seriously either," threw back Fellers.

"Mayor," pleaded Leroy, "this is still the Pickle Forge Police station and I think we otta..."

"Forget it Leroy," interrupted Jean. "Special Agent Butters is in charge here and we're going to follow her lead."

"Yeah Caderette," added Fellers, "you ain't a real cop! You only play at it three days a week and you spend most of those polishing parking meters or stuffing your fat face."

"Hey that's not fair, Bud, I'm a cop," bristled Leroy. "I'm Buzz's deputy."

Bud took a deep drag on his cigarette and blew the smoke in Caderette's direction. "If you're his deputy, then where were you while he was getting his fucking neck snapped?"

"Lay off him Fellers," snapped Jones. "Why do you always have to be such a horse's ass?"

"Nobody was talking to you Corky. Stick to your pathetic word-butchering and butt out."

"Damnit, that's enough you two!" blurted Jean. "Bud, you know that Leroy was helping Agent Butters. We've got a real problem here and bickering among ourselves isn't going to help solve it." Jean sucked on her own cigarette and then turned to Mickey. "Agent Butters, what should we do?"

Mickey felt like the proverbial deer caught in the headlights. "My first name is Kitrina mam, but I go by Mickey. Just call me Mickey."

"Ok Mickey," smiled Jean, "what do you think we should do?"

"Well, Mayor Rudolph..."

"Now wait a minute," interrupted Jean. "If you're Mickey, then I'm Jean. Let's all drop the formality shit."

"Fair enough Jean," nodded Mickey. "I called and, after a few tries, managed to leave a recorded message with my FBI field office in Portland. I also followed that up with a priority email. Unfortunately, it's total chaos back there. Until they get control of those bombings, I don't think we can expect any further help from the FBI's direction. I did, however, get through to the County Sheriff's office in Bend. They're swamped there too, but they think they can free up a couple of officers by midday tomorrow. That's the good news. The bad news is that, best case scenario, they won't be able to get here for at least another thirty-six hours."

"So where does that leave us," asked Jean looking troubled.

Mickey shrugged. "Until then, I think we had better just sit tight."

"Just sit tight! Wow, that's some pretty impressive leadership!" grumbled Fellers. "I say, I go down to my gas station and get Claude, then we pick up some boys from the Elks Lodge and we go after that murdering son-of-a-bitch."

"Whoa, hold your horses there, Bud!" protested Jean, holding out a hand in the universal sign for stop. "Things around here are bad enough without a bunch of gun toting drunks stirring up the pot."

"So we're just gonna sit in here and do nothing?"

"Bud, I'm not going to turn this town over to you and a crew of tipsy vigilantes."

"Yeah, that's a terrible idea," added Corky, "but still four people are dead! I think Bud's right. We can't just sit on our hands. We need to do something."

Jean again looked at Butters. "Mickey?"

Mickey's hands felt sweaty and a flock of doubts zoomed around inside her head like panicked starlings in an old barn. *Sure, I'm a trained FBI agent, but I'm not really trained for anything like this. Why the hell did Smallwood ever send me out here? I was supposed to back Edgar up. Now he's dead. I'm useless. They're all waiting for me to say something.* "Uhh..."

Before anything else could stumble out of her mouth, Leroy raised his hand like an excited student waiting to be called on in grade school. "Hey, hows about we go door to door and warn everyone to stay inside?"

Thank you! thought Mickey seizing on the idea. "Sure, Leroy, a door to door canvass could work. We don't need to tell people what's really going on. We just say that there's a rabid dog or something and that they all need to stay inside until we can get things sorted out."

"While we're at it," suggested Leroy, "we can tell 'em we're also looking for a transient who broke into Jean's barn. You know, ask if they've seen anyone suspicious."

Jean mulled it over. "It's Sunday so things will already be pretty quiet anyway. It just might work."

Feeling herself on firmer ground, Mickey looked at the others. "I think it's a good practical plan. Do you all agree?" One by one, they nodded their assent. Bud Fellers was last.

"Ok, that's it then," she continued taking firmer charge, "Jean, you work west from here with Bud and Corky. Leroy and I'll work east. It'll probably take us most of the day, but at least we'll be doing something positive and proactive."

Nearly ten hours later, with dusk once again approaching, Mickey stepped down off of a rickety porch and walked toward the Crown Vic where it sat on a rough gravel drive rampant with weeds. "Well, I think that's the last one," declared Leroy.

"For whatever good it did," sighed Mickey. "I'm not used to pulling all-nighters any more. I'm exhausted."

"I'm tired too," answered Leroy. "We didn't learn anything, but at least most folks took it without a fuss and they seem to be staying indoors. I know it ain't much but at least it's something. I think it was worth the effort."

"I suppose you're right," conceded Mickey. "I guess now we should head back over to the town hall."

Leroy paused by the door of the Vic. "You know Agent Butters, I've been thinking. Since nobody we talked to has seen or heard anything maybe we otta wander over to Gracie's Café or to the States Motel. It's a cinch that we're not after a local and any strangers who hit town usually wind up at one place or the other."

"I don't know Leroy, our guy's a multiple murderer on the run. I doubt that he's going to grab a quick bite or take a nap."

"Well, yeah," admitted Leroy, "but maybe somebody over at Gracie's or at the States saw him yesterday or something."

"I think it's a long shot, and Jean and the others are probably already waiting for us."

"Aw come on Agent Butters," wheedled Leroy. "Let's do some detecting."

Mickey smiled at his eagerness. "Oh hell, Deputy, I guess I've got a few miles left in my tank. It can't hurt. I'll call the others and let them know what we're going to do."

"Now you're talking," enthused Leroy. "My stomach is feeling pretty empty. Let's start with Gracie's."

Chapter 12

Whoever originally built The Fork and Spoon Café laid its foundation about halfway between the States Motel and downtown so that their new business could draw customers from both directions. Sitting out by itself, the venerable old eatery resembled an isolated island of light somehow afloat in the darkness. Bright fluorescents lit the café from the inside, but outside its windows the hungry night quickly consumed and devoured their glow.

Gracie Young ran a damp washrag over an already-clean counter that she'd, by now, wiped a dozen times before. *Well damn, if today don't beat all,* she mused. Then, she put down the rag and walked over by the windows to stare into her empty parking lot. *Sunday's supposed to be my big day! I'm supposed to get the after-church breakfast crowd. I only stay open late so ranchers can treat their wives to a Sunday meal! So how many customers do I get today? Six! That's how many! All because stuck-up ole Jean Rudolph and that fat white-boy, Leroy*

Caderette, been running around shooting their mouths off about a rabid dog or some such bullshit! Turning away in disgust, Gracie picked up her rag and headed back toward the kitchen. *Might as well just close her up. The way today's gone, staying open ain't going to make me one twig richer.*

Gracie had scarcely used her griddle all day, but her well-worn adage was, "Take care of your kitchen and it'll take care of you." She turned on the griddle to heat it a little, then slipped on her heat-resistant gloves. Once the surface warmed, Gracie carefully scrapped it clean of non-existent bits of food debris and grease. She'd just started scrubbing with a non-abrasive pad when the tiny bell over the café's front door gave out with its familiar clatter. In the unusual silence of the café, the unexpected sound made her jump. "Oh hell, I should have locked-up," she muttered. Shaking off her goosebumps, she removed her gloves, pulled on a clean apron and pinned her nametag back in place. *Might as well,* she thought, *a dollar's a dollar.*

Gracie peeped out over the kitchen pass-through. The customer was a man by himself and he'd already seated himself at one of the curved booths away from the windows. She shrugged to herself, grabbed a menu and a napkin-wrapped set of silverware, and hurried out of the kitchen. "Hi there sugar, haven't ever seen you in here before."

"Why, that's because I haven't been in here before," smiled the man. "Of course if I'd known my waitress was going to be so good looking, I'd have shown up a whole lot sooner."

Okay, so he's a flirt, thought Gracie. *Well I can do that too.* "Well listen to you, handsome and sweet to boot."

"Just telling the truth gorgeous, if the service here is half as good as your looks I'm in for a real treat. Honesty's my best trait."

"Oh, I doubt it's your best trait. I bet you've got all kinds of hidden attributes," quipped Gracie feeling blood rush to her cheeks at her own innuendo. *Be careful,* she thought.

"Maybe one," laughed the man with a smile lighting his face, but "that's only for special occasions." Taking the menu from her hand, he lightly brushed her fingers. He might have glanced at the offerings before he set the list aside, but to Gracie it seemed as if his eyes never left her face. He just sat there and stared.

His eyes, they're so beautiful! She felt herself falling into their shiny enticing depths. "This occasion might be special," she stammered. "Do you know what you want?"

"What would you recommend for someone like me?"

Gracie felt a sheen of perspiration spread across her face. Her heart raced and she shuddered with the pulse of the artery in her neck. "How about a slice of my own special pie?" *Dear God,* she thought. *Did I really say that?*

"You think I'd like it?" grinned the man, his eyes still never leaving her face.

"Oh you'll like it darling. It's moist and it's already warm." Gracie moaned. *What the fuck is happening to me? Why am I talking like this to a man I don't even know? What kind of harlot am I?*

"Sounds good," said the man sliding out of the booth and getting gracefully to his feet. "I've got a real deep hunger for something off the menu."

In a stupor, Gracie took the man's hand and slowly led him back through the kitchen. Continuing past the pantry, she unlatched the Fork and Spoon's back door and held it open. Once again, words that belonged to someone else, spewed from her mouth. "I've got something real tasty simmering. Why don't you come to my place out back and I'll dish you up a man-size helping."

"Oh, Gracie my dear, you have no idea," purred the man as he took a painful grip on her upper arm and propelled her out into the night.

When the high-beam headlights of the Vic swept across the empty parking lot, they illuminated a café that to Mickey's mind, jumped right out of the 1950's. "The place is lit up, but it looks pretty dead," she doubted. "You sure it's worth a stop?"

"Gracie Young might not have any leads for us," smiled Leroy, "but she makes the best damn biscuits and gravy in three states. I don't know about you, but my stomach's been growling for hours.

Mulling it over, Mickey, was forced to admit that she too was really hungry. In fact, now that she thought about it, she couldn't remember when she last ate. *We're kind of spinning our wheels, I suppose a sandwich or something isn't such a bad idea.* Nodding agreement, she directed the Vic to a gravelly stop by the café's front door and shut off the motor. "Okay, I could eat something," she admitted. "Lead on."

Leroy held the door. *A gentleman,* thought Mickey and stepped inside. Her first impression was the same as it had been from the parking lot. *Straight out of the 50's* and also *Wow! This is really cute!* Her second impression was that the café was spotlessly clean and deserted, no customers and no one behind the counter.

Leroy stepped in close behind her. "Gracie?"

Mickey raised her voice a bit, "Hello, is anyone here?"

"Maybe she's in her place out back," offered Leroy. "She does that sometimes when business is really slow. If the front door is open, most of her regulars just head for the kitchen and rustle their own grub until she shows up."

Mickey frowned, "Ok, let's try out back."

"Sure, but first let's grab some pie. I'm really hungry," begged Leroy.

"Let's just finish here and move on. I called, but the others are going to be waiting at city hall for us to turn up."

"Oh come on Agent Butters. I'm starving. It'll only take a few minutes, then we'll wander around back. We haven't eaten anything since this morning; aren't you feeling hungry? You said you could eat."

Mickey rolled her eyes. "Drop the 'Agent Butters' shtick and I'll consider it. Is the pie here any good?"

"Oh my God," gushed Leroy walking behind the counter. "Gracie's pies make her biscuits and gravy want to hide in shame. You sit down at the counter and I'll serve us up.

Feeling a bit naughty, Mickey sat down at one of the counter stools as Leroy pulled a couple of extra-large slices of pie from a big glass case next to the kitchen pass-thru. "You look like an all-American kind of gal. You're going to love Gracie's apple pie it's to die for!" Leroy set one slice in front of Mickey and the other in front of the stool next to her. Reaching under the counter, he then produced napkin-wrapped silverware that he set down by the plates.

The pie looked delicious. Salivating, Mickey hurriedly unwrapped her fork. She was just about to dig in when Leroy held up his hand to stop, "Oh no, not yet, wait!" Then, he hustled off into the kitchen. Moments later, he reemerged clutching an industrial-size container of whipped cream. Aiming it at Mickey's plate, he smothered her pie. "Okay, now it's the full experience. Go for it!"

As he came around the counter and slipped onto the stool next to her, Mickey popped a fork-full into her mouth. "Mmmmm, this is great! I guess I'm hungrier than I thought."

"Didn't I tell you?" declared Leroy confidently. For several minutes, they just sat silently enjoying their pie, then Leroy set down his fork and turned on his stool. "Mickey, this might be prying or personal, but were you and Edgar close?"

The question surprised Mickey, but it didn't put her off. "It's okay Leroy, I don't think you're prying. I suppose I got along with Ed well enough. Honestly I barely knew him. I just started working at the

Portland bureau office. Our desks were near to each other, but we weren't buddies or anything. Close? No we weren't close. Until this assignment, I bet we hadn't spoken more than a dozen times. Ed was old school and he never really got what I do. I think maybe he was married you know, but I didn't met her. How about you and Buzz?"

"I know he's dead," sighed Leroy. "I saw him lying there. You and I wrapped him in that damn plastic, but well, it's still not real yet. I still expect him to pull up in his truck and swagger through that door. I knew him forever. We grew up together."

Mickey looked into his eyes, "I'm really sorry man. It's been a truly shitty day."

"Buzz liked me. I don't know why," continued Leroy. "He was always the captain of the team and I was always the chubby kid who got picked last. For some reason, he always stood by me and he treated me like a somebody. You know what I do for a living?"

"No I guess not."

"I'm part-time janitor at the Pickle's Forge grade school. Kids all used to make fun of me before Buzz asked me to be his deputy."

Mickey reached over and patted his hand. "He picked a good man Leroy Caderette."

Leroy sniffled a couple of times and then wiped his nose with his napkin. "I know I'm not a real cop like you, but getting to work with Buzz made me feel like one."

Not a real cop like you. The words almost knocked Mickey off her stool. "Leroy, I feel like a fraud," she blurted "I told you that I just started working at the Portland field office. The truth is, I haven't worked anywhere else. I've only been a special agent for a few weeks. Sure, I had all the proper training, but this is my first time out in the field. The FBI is something I've worked toward since I was twelve, but that's not the same as experience. I'm supposed to be an expert on Internet bad guys, cyber creeps. I'm supposed to be sitting in front of a computer, not in the middle of nowhere chasing some murderous psychopath. My agent in charge only sent me along with Ed because there was no one else available. I was supposed to be his backup. Now, he's dead. The Inspection Division is going to take one look at what I've done out here, and that's the end of my career. I don't know what to do. I never thought I'd be on my own like this. I always thought that I'd be part of a team. I'm scared that someone else will get hurt because of my incompetence."

Now it was Leroy's turn to reach out and pat a hand. "I don't know what to do either, Agent Butters. I'm scared too, but we're sort of a team. We just have to hold it together until tomorrow when the cavalry arrives. You're smart and you're brave, and you're FBI. I'll follow where you lead. We'll do the best we can." Mickey smiled and nodded.

Chapter 13

Gideon's head felt like perhaps it wasn't his own, or as though someone had stuffed it full of old brown paper bags. He shook it carefully from side to side and stared warily about. To his bewilderment, he was standing in a small neat living room, one that was deeply shrouded in darkness: a worn overstuffed couch with an oval coffee table, an armchair with doilies on both arms, a television set on a metal stand, and a painting of Baby Jesus hanging on the far wall.

Where in the world am I? he wondered. *How did I ever get here?* In the midst of those thoughts he abruptly felt the pull. Just as suddenly, he realized that he was clutching his spear and his duffle bag. *The pull is almost never this strong.* In that instant, understanding brought him fully awake. *The demon! He's here! Why is it always like this, like waking from a dream?* Time and time again, Gideon would open his eyes with no memory of how he arrived somewhere, and by some divine miracle find himself wherever it was that his God needed him most.

The neat compact room held only two doors. Instinctively, he knew that the one just behind his back led to the outside. The other door was shut tight. Even so, he sensed the powerful evil that lurked behind it. Taking a firmer grip on his spear, he stepped forward. Slowly he turned the knob, and shoved the door wide open. From uncomfortable experience Gideon knew roughly what to expect. Still, the scene that met his eyes took him aback and filled him with an aching melancholy.

A large, double, wood-framed glass door looked out of the room onto spectral woods and blue-white moonlight poured through the door's farmhouse style panes. Bathed in the ghostly light, the perpetually well-dressed demon stood on the near-side of a rumpled twin bed. Slightly hunched over, he effortlessly supported the body of an unconscious woman clad in only her underwear. The woman's head lolled back and the demon pressed his lips against her throat. Blood, black as ink in the moonlight, dripped down her chest, slithered across her stomach, and pooled onto the floor.

As Gideon inched through the door, the fiend glanced up, angry red eyes flared in the darkness. "Ah Mister Robinson, inopportunely here at last. I wondered when you'd arrive. Buzz-kill as ever; have you come to do good deeds and smite the wicked?"

"It's the Lord who punishes the wicked and the lascivious," whispered Gideon. "I only do his bidding."

The demon nonchalantly dumped the senseless woman onto the bed and gave his uninvited guest his full attention. "Do you always have to be so predictable and droll? I intend to keep this one and I grow increasingly bored with your countless, although ineffectual, interruptions. How often are we to play this preposterous game?"

"As often as it takes, Demon! We play until you're burning in hell where you belong," yelled Gideon. Dropping his duffle, he lunged forward with his spear outstretched. He put all of his considerable strength and weight behind the brutal thrust. The demon didn't move, but it was almost as though he was never there. Gideon's blade cleaved thin air. With nothing to resist his vicious attack, he staggered forward, stumbled and slammed into a wall.

"Thank you Satan!" cackled the monster. "This is the part that I truly enjoy!"

Shaky and unsteady, Gideon struggled back on to his feet. His nemesis gloated mere paces away. Gideon dodged to his right. Eyes never leaving the beast, he swung the razor-sharp edge of his spear, again with all his might. It wasn't possible the cruel blade could miss. Still, miss it did. The demon held his belly with both hands and roared with crazed laughter as the heavy spear buried itself into the top of an old pine chest of drawers.

As Gideon struggled to wrench free his stubbornly trapped weapon, the laughing fiend scooped the woman back into his arms. Then, amid a shower of glass, he smashed through the double doors carrying her away.

"No!" screamed Gideon. "Noooo!" Muscles straining, he wrenched loose his trapped spear. With his free hand he grabbed up his discarded bag and then, oblivious to the broken door's sharp jagged shards, he plunged through it in pursuit.

Chapter 14

Mickey and Leroy finished their lip-smacking slices of pie and Leroy washed their plates and silverware before they strolled out the café's back door. A few steps away, along a neatly tended gravel path, a dim flickering porch light tried to illuminate the front of a small nondescript cottage. Two small windows gave no hint as to its darkened interior, but for the briefest of moments Mickey, thought that a deeper shadow might have moved across the one on the left.

"Did you just hear something?" she asked, perhaps imagining the muffled sounds of some sort of commotion.

"Not me," said Leroy, rapping softly on the door. "Hey Gracie, you in there?" After a pause with no response, he knocked a bit harder. The door, which he'd expected to be securely latched, swung open with a tiny squeak. He threw Mickey a worried stare. "I don't like this. It's vintage Gracie to hang out back here, but it ain't like her, even one little bit, to leave her door unlatched."

Mickey, nodded and drew her gun. "Okay, let's be careful." Leroy drew his own firearm and used his toe to slowly push in the door until it was fully open. "Gracie?" Cautiously, Mickey edged past.

"Missus Young, can you hear me? This is the FBI. There are two law officers out here and we're about to enter your home." Again there was no response.

"This is really weird," whispered Leroy, "and it makes me pretty frigging nervous."

"Okay," answered Mickey. "I get it, but we still need to go in. I'll go first. You come in behind me, but don't get freaked and shoot me in the back."

Six careful steps later, they both stood in the cottage's darkened living room. Leroy tried again, "Gracie?"

Then Mickey, "FBI! Mam, can you hear us?"

Silence answered them back. Uneasy, they nodded to each other and then moved quietly toward the room's only other door. Unlike the front door, that one was firmly closed. Mickey lightly grasped the knob and stared pointedly at Leroy and put a finger to her lips. "We don't know what we're going to find. She might just be sound asleep. We go through the door in a rush, but no cowboy stuff. Be ready, but be careful. On three; one, two, three!"

With Mickey's hard shove, the hollow-core door swung wide open with a muffled "bang." Bending low, as she'd been taught, with her automatic held in front of her, she dove into the room. Leroy rushed in, hard on her heels. The room was every bit as dark and silent as the one they'd just left. Immediately, they both stopped in surprise.

Weak moonlight seeped in through a shattered wooden and glass door, but it revealed little. "Lights?" whispered Mickey, and Leroy flicked a switch on the wall. A fallen pole lamp that lay on the floor burst into a flickering radiance, and the light that poured from beneath its crushed shade presented a compact scene of wanton destruction.

"Holy Shit!" groaned Leroy. Then, Mickey spotted the blood, dark thick blood splattered on the bed, congealing blood pooled on the floor.

Oh God! Oh God! I'm standing in it! The gun slipped slowly out of her hand and the room began to darken and spin. She gagged and staggered a step into Leroy. As he stumbled awkwardly backwards, FBI Special Agent Kitrina Butters coughed once and crumpled into a heap on a dry part of the floor.

Chapter 15

The demon stood statuesque among dirt clods in the middle of a recently cleared field. Bathed in the radiance of the ascendant moon, he gave the impression of an actor in the glow of lime lights about to speak his lines on some cosmic stage. In the distance the nighttime lights of Pickle's Forge sparkled, pathetic and wane in their comparison. Fastidiously, the wraith brushed a few grains of soil from his immaculate cashmere coat. Gracie Lee's semi-nude, blood-smeared, body hung carelessly across his shoulder. Not a single drop of her precious blood spoilt his spotless ensemble. With a sigh, he slowly turned and faced about.

Gideon crouched mere paces away. The demon's gaze slowly took him in noting the disappointing contrast. Gideon's clothes were torn and bloodstained, *a disgusting shambles*. His face, hands, and arms were cut from the glass of the broken door and oozing blood. Still, he clutched tightly to his spear and circled, edging closer.

"You know, Robinson," hissed the demon, "you really are a huge, and I mean enormous, pain in my ass. Whenever I start to have even the tiniest bit of fun, here you come tramping about with your stupid spear and your self-righteous talk about sin. I've just about had it with you. I think perhaps your time in this benighted world is short."

"You don't scare me fiend," quavered Gideon. "You know that I'm stronger than you. You know that you fear me. My strength comes from the lord!"

"Oh spare me," chuckled the deceiver. "Do you know how insanely ridiculous you sound? Insane, there's a good term. Think about what you're doing, Robinson! Are your thoughts and actions those of a sane person?"

Gideon edged closer. "Give me the woman."

"Every party needs a pooper, but I don't recall inviting you," laughed the demon. Then, he hoisted Gracie off his shoulder and stood her up facing Gideon. Giggling, he slipped his hand under her bra and caressed her breasts. "Yes, yes, you'd like her wouldn't you?" he chortled. "I can see it in your eyes. You want her for yourself. Oh wait! Maybe you already have her! What are you going to do with her? Nothing sordid I hope."

"Just give her to me fiend," screamed Gideon. "You've stolen her soul but I won't let you keep it."

"No, perhaps not," responded the unclean spirit with a wry smile. "Yet, the night is still quite young and there are plenty of other fish in the sea. Here; I wanted this one, but you can have her. I'm throwing her back."

With that, the smiling fiend hurled Gracie's insensate body into Gideon knocking him to his knees in the plowed dirt. When he looked up, he and Gracie were alone. "This is the last one," he breathed. "I swear it is, monster. Wherever you go I'll be there. You won't escape me again." Then, with weary resignation, he unzipped his duffle bag containing its grim cargo of hammer and spikes.

Chapter 16

Mickey slowly swam back to awareness and was disconcerted to discover herself slumped in the passenger seat of the Crown Vic. The car was still parked in the gravel lot in front of the Fork and Spoon, and the building's florescent lights still shown out into the darkness. The Vic's dome light illuminated its interior, and Leroy was speaking earnestly into an older flip-phone.

"Just like I said, Jean, it looks real bad. Gracie's not in her house and the place is all busted up. There's blood on her bedroom floor. Somebody broke out her glass backdoor."

Leroy paused and Mickey straightened up, shaking her head from side to side to clear the last of the cobwebs. "Yeah, we looked there, out back too," he continued. Leroy stopped talking again, then he threw Mickey a kind of hopeless shrug, and handed her the phone.

"Yes, Jean, this is Mickey. Unhuh, Leroy is right, it doesn't look good. I'm pretty sure your Gracie's been abducted. If she has, I seriously doubt that she'll last until morning."

After listening to Jean's response, she frowned. "No, we need more help right away. It's against all my better judgement, but I think it's time for the drunks with guns. Why don't you, Bud, and Corky find as many armed volunteers as you can, explain to them what's really going on, and meet us out here at The Fork and Spoon in say thirty minutes." She paused, then ended the call saying, "Ok, but try to get them here as quickly as you can. Mickey out." She closed the phone with a click and handed it back.

"Leroy, I'm really disoriented. How did I get here?"

Leroy looked awkward. "You fainted. I tried to wake you up, but you were out cold. I wasn't sure what else to do, so I carried you here to the car. It was just easier to get you into the passenger seat. I had to dig around in your pockets for your keys. I'm sorry."

"Jesus, there's nothing to be sorry about. I'm the one who should be sorry. You did great! I'm FBI, but you're the one who's doing everything right. Oh shit! What must Jean and the others think of me?"

"I didn't tell 'em," whispered Leroy. "There's no reason that they need to know what happened. You're smart and you're trained, and they need to have confidence in you."

"But for pity's sake, what about you? You saw what happened to me. You had to carry me out here to the damn car."

"I've got confidence in you Mickey," nodded Leroy. "Yeah, your fainting was some scary shit, but it wasn't anything that you coulda helped. What's more, I know that it doesn't mean diddly squat about your qualifications to be the one in charge here. What went down back there is just between you and me, and that's how it stays."

"Leroy, are you sure that you want to keep it that way?"

"You're in charge," he repeated. "So what's our next move?"

"Jean said that she'll round up a coalition of the willing," answered Mickey, "but also that it might take a bit to get them moving."

"I'm not going to second guess you," apologized Leroy, "but you were still a little woozy when I gave you the phone. Do you really think volunteers are a good idea? You don't know Bud Fellers like I do. We're more likely to end up with an armed lynch mob than a posse."

"I think it's a risk that we have to take, Leroy. No outside help is gonna be here until morning and you and I can't go this alone. If we want to have a chance in hell of finding Gracie before it's too late, Bud and his guys will have to do."

"Fair enough, so what do we do until they get here?" quizzed Leroy.

"Since we have some time, I think we need to go out back again to Gracie's cottage. We might see something useful, some hint as to where he's taken her. It was mostly the surprise that caught me off guard. Now that I'm expecting it, I think I can handle the blood." Just saying it out loud made Mickey feel slightly nauseous.

Leroy once again looked sheepish. "I'm no FBI agent like you," he muttered, "but I already checked and I'm pretty sure there's nothing back there that can help us."

"You already checked?" asked Mickey looking both surprised and serious. "When did you have time to do that?"

"Well, I looked around after I put you in the car. You were breathing normally, and didn't seem in any way distressed, so I just locked you in and headed back there."

Mickey stared at Leroy with a modicum of new found respect. "Really, you went back there by yourself?"

"You seemed okay, and I thought it was the right thing to do. I looked really carefully, but I didn't touch nothing."

"Yes, yes, that's good." *He's not trained; he might have missed something,* thought Mickey, but then she thought again about all of the blood. "Alright Leroy, if you've already searched thoroughly, there's no point in us doing it again. I guess we wait." Feeling both relieved and guilty, Mickey got out of the car and stretched. "Slide out from behind the wheel and let's switch places."

Leroy immediately got out and walked around to the passenger seat. Mickey climbed in and pulled out her iPhone. She gave the screen an anxious look and then started to fiddle. The phone emitted a slight glow and a series of quiet clicks as she double thumbed its virtual keypad. Leroy sat patiently and waited, but after a couple of minutes he began to feel restless.

"You know Mickey, I feel like we shouldn't just sit here. I think we should be doing something."

"I am doing something," she retorted with a frown. "I'm making notes for my investigation report."

"Naw, I mean something active. If we've got a whole half hour before Jean and Bud can show, why don't we roll up the highway to the States Motel and give it a quick eyeball?"

"We've got the time, and that's not the worst idea," said Mickey, "but this is a crime scene. We really shouldn't just leave."

"It ain't going nowhere. Let's just put on Gracie's "closed" sign, turn out the lights, and shut the door.

We do that, and no one'll stop and mess with anything."

"I don't know," responded Mickey. "If anyone at my field office ever hears that I left a crime scene without fully securing it I'll get my ass chewed and then be reassigned to the South Pole."

"Aw come on, nobody in Portland is going to find out. You start driving and I'll call Jean and fill her in on what's up."

Chapter 17

After a short drive, the Vic rolled into the parking lot of the rundown cottage style motel. A neon sign reading "Office" glowed against a building at one end so Mickey pulled to a stop out front. She and Leroy both climbed out, and he held the door as they entered the office.

The States Motel's teen-age night clerk looked up with a start, and hurriedly shoved something that he was reading away out of sight. Then, he recognized Leroy and his startled expression changed to a sly grin. He took a deep drag on a cigarette that hung from his lips and blew a half-assed smoke ring across the counter while he carefully appraised Mickey. "Howdy LC," he drawled. "What brings you out this time of night? Are you and your cutie there looking for an hourly room?" Mickey blushed a little, and the cocky clerk guffawed loudly at what he considered a hysterical joke.

"Stow it Kim," snapped Leroy. "This is official police business. This here's Special Agent Kitrina

Butters of the FBI." Mickey flashed her badge and the clerk leaned closer, looking impressed.

"No shit! For real?" he gushed. "That's way cool! What's the FBI doing way out here in Pickle's Forge? Oh, oh, wow, you're after the towel heads that done the bombing aren't ya?"

"Something like that," deflected Mickey. "What time did you come on duty, Kim?"

"Always the same time, every Sunday, Tuesday, and Thursday," he responded. "Five o'clock, that's when my shift starts, five sharp."

"Have things been quiet?" asked Leroy.

"Yeah, I suppose," answered Kim, taking another drag on his cigarette.

"Nothing out of the ordinary, no strangers?" queried Mickey.

"Well, there's that old black guy, Smith, down ta unit eight. I ain't seen him but Herb said he checked in day before yesterday."

Mickey and Leroy exchanged a look and Kim, catching the expressions that passed between them, hurried excitedly on. "No car or luggage, just an old duffle, Herb said he just wandered in and paid cash. Is he wanted? Ya think he's one of the bombers?"

"Where's unit eight?" demanded Mickey.

"Down ta the far end."

"Okay, I know you've got an extra key for the room," said Leroy. "Hand it over."

"Wait a minute, you want in?" clucked Kim. "I've got a spare key, but I don't think I should give it to you. Our guests here at the States have rights. Have you got a warrant or anything?"

"What I've got," growled Leroy, "is a mind to come behind that counter and ring your skinny neck. Now hand it over."

"Hey, don't get all worked up. I was just saying." Kim reached behind himself, took a key attached to an eight-inch piece of 1x2 off a rack on the wall and held it out to Mickey. "You gonna to arrest him?"

"No," she responded, "we're just going to talk." With that, Mickey and Leroy turned and headed for the door. Kim immediately jumped up and hurried around the counter to follow."

"Whoa! Slow down there cowboy," objected Leroy holding up his hand. "You ain't going nowhere."

"That's right son," added Mickey. You need to stay right here."

Kim watched Caderette and the FBI gal step out of the office and close its door behind them. "I never get any fun," he whined. "This job sucks!"

Chapter 18

Room number eight, at the end of a cracked concrete walkway, was situated farthest from the office. The yellow glow of its dim porch light was attracting moths and other insects, but the room itself appeared dark. Standing side by side in front of its door, Leroy turned to Mickey. "So how do we play this?"

"Very carefully," she answered. "Walking, going light on luggage, and paying with cash aren't crimes. We knock and if he's in we're official and polite. If no one answers, we knock louder. Then, if there's still no answer we let ourselves in and have a quick look around."

Shortly, following Mickey's soft knock, a light came on somewhere back behind the room's drawn window curtains. After a moment, she knocked again and the security peephole in the door went dark.

"Who's out there?" asked someone from inside the room.

Mickey held up her badge where it could be seen. "I'm a federal officer Mr. Smith we'd like to speak with you."

The door opened a crack, safety chain in place, and a man peered out. From what Mickey could see, the man was African American. He appeared well groomed, and he was wearing some sort of old work uniform. His face seemed pleasant and open.

"Yes, officers, what's this about?"

"We'd just like a minute of your time, answered Mickey, still holding up her credentials. I'm FBI Special Agent Kitrina Butters and this is Officer Leroy Caderette. "Do you mind if we come in?"

The man looked wary and uncertain. "I was just about to crawl into bed."

"We promise we won't keep you long," offered Leroy.

"You officers aren't going to just go away are you?" asked the man.

"No sir we're not," smiled Mickey

"Oh well, then you better come in," he gave a resigned sigh and reached to unlatch the safety chain. Once the door was free, the man held it open.

With a broad inviting smile, he stepped politely back and gestured them in. Leroy took the lead. As he stepped past, Mickey appraised the man again, *Middle-aged, six one or six two, maybe 230 pounds.*

She didn't have time for another thought. As she followed Leroy into the room, the man suddenly spun from his spot by the door swinging some sort of, previously concealed, wooden rod. Before Mickey could even start to react, the hardened shaft connected with the back of her head. A solid resounding "CRACK" echoed in the room and she went down like she'd been tackled by a linebacker.

Startled by the sound, Leroy immediately spun around. His eyes went wide. "Hey!" he yelled, and fumbled to draw his gun. Before he managed to free the weapon from its holster, the man charged. The butt of the wooden rod rammed forcefully into Leroy's gut. Doubling over in pain, he grunted, and struggled catch his breath. The man struck him again and abruptly he joined Mickey face down on the floor.

Leroy's gun clattered free and the man looked down and kicked it away. "I'm sorry," he apologized.

"I didn't want to hurt either of you, but you can't interfere. You don't know. You don't understand his power. I'm the only one who can stop him. He won't spare you." Without another word, the man reversed his deadly spear and hurried out of the room.

Leroy coughed a couple of times and struggled to his hands and knees. He then crawled across the floor to where Mickey sprawled unmoving. "Oh shit, Mickey, Mickey," he wheezed are you still with me? Come on wake up." She groaned softly and, straining a bit, he managed to lift her up and carefully lay her on the bed. Moments later, as he dabbed her face with a wet washcloth, she began to come around.

"Whaa what happened?"

"Oh thank God," mumbled Leroy as he helped her sit up. "I was worried. That bastard hit you so hard I thought he might have really busted your skull."

Carefully, Mickey raised her right hand to the back of her head and winced. When she lowered the hand, it was spotted with red. Horror registered across her face and her eyes began to flutter.

"Shit!" exclaimed Leroy, hurrying to hold her up. "Stay with me! None of that; you're going to be fine." Mickey swayed a little but remained conscious and upright. "Okay, see that's better," he soothed. "Here, wipe your hand on this," he urged, handing her the washcloth. "Let me look at your head." She bent down some and Leroy gently moved her hair a little. "It's just a tiny scalp cut," he said, sounding relieved. "They always bleed a lot, but it's already stopped oozing. Let me rinse that cloth and I'll clean you up a bit."

Mickey sat quietly on the edge of the bed while Leroy worked. "There," he said when finished. "It might still sting for a while, but, barring a concussion, you should be fine. You're lucky, when I saw you hit the floor, you looked like you had gone down for the count."

"God I'm sorry, Leroy," sighed Mickey. "FBI agent, what a joke. I'm nothing but a poser."

"Bullshit, he suckered us both. You never stood a chance. Neither of us was ready for anything like that."

"Yeah, but I should have been! I saw his big friendly smile, forgot all my weeks of training, and just walked into it. I ought to just give up and get a job waiting tables like I did in college."

"It was him; wasn't it, Special Agent Butters?" asked Leroy emphasizing Special Agent.

"Yeah," answered Mickey with a weary grin. "It had to be! But, I never got a good look at him in the junkyard."

"I didn't either, but the thing he hit us with was the shaft of that big spear he used on Mary Beth. I saw it clearly before he ran. Why do you think he let the two of us live?"

"That's the hundred dollar question of the hour. Your guess is as good as mine."

"Think you're feeling well enough to move around?" asked Leroy. "You're not still dizzy are you?"

"No, I'm not dizzy," answered Mickey. "My head's throbbing a little, but I think I'm ok. I'm more mortified than hurt. We're wasting time. Let's toss this room and get after him. You check around in the bathroom and I'll check in here."

Chapter 19

Shortly, after finishing their quick search of the room, Mickey and Leroy climbed back into the Crown Vic and headed toward The Fork and Spoon. Leroy hunkered behind the steering wheel. On the backseat lay two large clear evidence bags. A wad of bloody clothes was visible inside one. The other held an expensive elongated leather case with brass clasps. Mickey sat, seat-belted, in the passenger seat, wearing a pair of nitrile gloves. Next to another evidence bag on her lap perched a nondescript grey duffle bag that she was closely examining. One by one, she removed each item the duffle contained, made a note in her phone and then placed the item into the third evidence bag.

"Wow! I can't believe that crap," snorted Leroy, glancing over, "iron stakes, a mallet, a whip, a roll of cash; Holy shit!"

"Shit is just about right," retorted Mickey, thumbing through an old dog-eared notebook. "That lunatic's been keeping a journal and this is the most demented thing that I've ever read. The FBI psych guys and profilers pegged him for a religious nut and, truth be told, there's a lot of mission-from-God kind of stuff in here. But, that's not the really crazy part. Leroy, this madman thinks he's hunting a vampire, a real vampire; you know, fangs, blood sucking, the whole works. He thinks he releases the creature's minions from damnation by chopping their heads off. It's sick. It's like he believes he's Vampire Hunter D or something!"

"Aw man, Gracie!" moaned Leroy. "He's gonna do her just like he did the others. We gotta get her back. We need to stop him."

"We will," asserted Mickey feigning a confidence that she didn't feel. "We'll do it, you and me."

Leroy swung the Vic off of the highway and into The Fork and Spoon's gravel lot. The space ahead was lit by the headlights of four pickup trucks and a couple of cars arranged into a rough ring. Milling about in the ring's center shuffled a small crowd of people and several dogs. Leroy pulled up and parked just outside the circle and he and Mickey got out. As soon as they had barely opened their doors they heard grumbling.

"It's them alright. About fucking time! Let's get to catching the bastard. Yeah, enough of this standing around bull, let's kick some ass!" These sentiments were met by irritated mutters of assent. The crowd was composed mostly of men. Some held rifles, one or two clutched tire irons. Assorted baseball bats were also in evidence. A couple of the men were unselfconsciously drinking from half empty liquor bottles.

As they approached, Leroy whispered quietly into Mickey's ear. "So, this still look like a good idea to you?"

Jean Rudolph, Bud Fellers, and Corky Jones stepped forward from the group. "Christ Almighty Mickey," gushed Jean, radiating concern. "What happened? Where were you? Why didn't you or Leroy call? We've been waiting nearly an hour!"

Corky Jones looked closely at Mickey. "You look a little peaky Agent Butters. Are you alright?

"I'm ok," answered Mickey. I got smacked in the head with a piece of wood. It left me a little woozy. We almost had him."

"Yeah," threw in Leroy, "he was right there at the States motel in unit number eight."

"So where the fuck is he now?" demanded Bud Fellers. "What the hell happened?"

"He's real fast," explained Leroy. "We stepped into his room to talk with him and he clubbed Mickey hard from behind. Then, he got the jump on me."

"Got the jump on you? That's rich! You're oh-for-two fat boy," crowed Fellers. "Whose back are you not going to be watching next time?" Murmurs of agreement and derision escaped from the crowd.

"Watch it Bud or else!" grimaced Leroy.

"Or else, or else what? You're hopeless Caderette," countered Fellers. Then to guffaws of laughter, "You couldn't catch fish with dynamite."

"So where'd he go after you let him escape?" barked someone from the crowd.

"We don't know for sure," admitted Mickey in response. "He just ran away."

"Well, if he's still out there on foot, he can't have gone far," offered Corky Jones.

"You heard 'em boys," bellowed Fellers, that murdering scum's out near the States Motel and he's running. Let's saddle up! Lock and load!" With whoops and hollers everyone began to pile into three of the pickups. Appalled, Mickey and Leroy urged them to stop. Nobody bothered to listen.

As Fellers opened the driver's door to one of the trucks, Jean Rudolph grabbed at his arm. "Bud, wait! Wait just a damn minute! Think this through!"

"Mister Fellers," pleaded Mickey, you can't just go rushing off. There's information about this suspect that you don't know. You need a plan! I can't authorize this action."

"We know everything we need to know! This murdering psycho is nearby and he's on foot. We have a plan; we're going to catch the bastard. And, we don't need the FBI's authorization to do it!" Slamming the door, Fellers turned his key in the truck's ignition and gunned its engine.

Jean looked up at Jones, who was wedged with other vigilantes into the back of the truck. "Corky, you know this isn't right!"

Pickle Forge's representative of the Fourth Estate stared back, spread his hands, and mouthed "What can I do?"

Fellers gunned his engine again and all three of the trucks tore off into the night with tires squealing and gravel spraying. Mickey, Leroy, and Jean stood alone next to the remaining vehicles and watched the pickups roar away. "Well, that didn't go so well," mused Leroy.

"I can't believe they just took off like that," snapped Mickey. "I needed to give them ground rules. Hell, none of them are even deputized!"

"Bud Fellers can be such a huge jerk," commiserated Jean. "If he wasn't on the city council, sometimes I don't think I'd even speak to him."

Mickey sighed, and held her hands to the sides of her head. "They just drove away. Now they're out there tearing around with guns and baseball bats. That woman, Carol Green, from the market, for Christ sake, she even had a pitchfork!"

"I tried to warn you," reminded Leroy.

Mickey grimaced, then walked over to the Vic and yanked open it driver's door. "Hop in, we need to get after them before someone gets hurt."

"Hang on a second," counseled Leroy.

"Why?"

"They're headed straight for the States Motel, right?"

"I guess so," acknowledged Mickey.

"Well then, we'll catch up to them there for sure."

"So?"

"So I'm thinking our investigating almost paid off earlier. We flubbed it, but we came close to catching him."

"Leroy, what are you running on about?" demanded Jean

"You can take your car Jean, and run straight up the highway to the States," he answered. "When you get there, talk to Bud. Try to convince him that we believe that the psycho's gone to ground. Persuade him that he and his boys need to fan out and do a foot search around the motel and the junction with Old Creek Road. Corky will probably back you up, and that should keep everyone busy and out of trouble until we get there.”

“So,” asked Mickey looking skeptical, “what exactly are you, Deputy Caderette, and I going to be doing while Mayor Rudolph here single handedly corrals Fellers and his lynch mob?”

Leroy smiled. “We’re going to be detecting!”

The Vic’s headlights carved a tunnel through the moonlit darkness outside, and Mickey was once again behind the wheel. “I’ll say one thing; it’s an awesome night for vampires, full moon and all that. Are you sure this road takes us back to the motel?”

“That’s werewolves,” smiled Leroy. “Full moons, those are for werewolves. Sure I’m sure; I’ve lived here my whole life.”

“Vampires, werewolves, whatever; it doesn’t feel like we’re headed in the right direction.”

“That’s because this old road winds way around to the north. It’ll get us to the States, but it twists and turns back on itself all higgledy-piggledy. It tracks a bunch of historic property lines.”

"And, tell me again why we're out here and not at the motel with Jean?"

"It's like I said," answered Leroy, our guy might be crazy as a rabid squirrel, but, just the same, he doesn't want to get caught. He's gonna stay away from the main highway. He's going to head for somewhere quieter, somewhere darker."

"Okay, I'll buy that, Leroy, but, why this road?"

"Like you Mickey, this loon is a first-time stranger to Pickle's Forge. He's not going to go cutting cross country because he doesn't wanta end up wandering around mixed up and lost. Naw, he'll stick to a backroad, and, if you start from the States Motel, this is the only one."

"I still don't like Jean off by herself, objected Mickey. "Jesus, this murderer we're after actually thinks he's hunting fucking vampires!"

"Don't worry about Jean," countered Leroy. "When her Irish is up, she's one tough lady. Bud and his boys'll look after her. Fellers doesn't always show it, but he thinks she's the bee's knees!"

Standing in front of the office door of the States Motel, Bud Fellers leaned far enough forward so that he pushed into the young night clerk's personal space. "Is that so Roberts? And you're sure?"

Kim Roberts, leaned away, glanced at the surly mob arrayed behind *that prick*, Fellers, and glared back. "I already told you! I didn't see nothing. Fat Leroy and that FBI lady made me stay in the office."

"Come on Kim," urged Corky Jones standing just behind Bud. "Think hard. This is important. You must remember something."

While Kim was humming and hawing, everyone suddenly looked away as Jean Rudolph pulled up in her 1963 Volvo and hopped out. With all eyes upon her, she stalked determinedly toward the group and began shoving her way to the front.

"Damn it Bobby Earl; Claude, move!"

"Now Jean, don't you start," warned Fellers giving her his attention. "We know what we're doing!"

"Is that so? In a pig's eye! You're all running around like stupid chickens with your heads cut off.

You need to stop acting the fool and listen for a minute!"

"All right Madam Mayor," glared Bud, "fine, we're listening. Say your piece."

"Where are Leroy and Agent Butters?" asked Corky Jones.

"They'll be along directly, Corky. Bud you and your posse aren't looking in the right place!"

"Whatta ya mean?" retorted Fellers. "This is where Caderette and the FBI gal saw him ain't it?"

"That's what I'm trying to tell you," threw back Jean. "Mickey and Leroy spotted him ducking into the trees and heading toward Old Creek Road. They would have gone after him right then, but they thought he would slip away if it was just the two of them."

"If they knew where he was hiding, why didn't they say nothing?"

"Why do you think Bud? Because, you and your heroes ran off half-cocked, without asking!"

Jean turned to the others, pointing. "Now listen up all of you! You need to get down there, on Old

Creek Road, spread out on each side of the pavement and start beating the brush!"

Bobby Earl and Claude turned to Fellers. Claude spoke, "What do you think Bud?"

Bud Fellers grinned. "I think you heard our mayor. Come on boys lets flush a rat!" With flashlights and a couple of blazing torches, everyone stalked off in the direction Jean had pointed.

Chapter 20

Gideon moved slowly and furtively through the pitch black screen of trees which lined the cracked pavement. His passage was silent and only small night sounds intruded on the stillness. *This is bad, he thought. I had to hurt those officers and I had to leave everything behind. I can't replace my things around here. Why did I ever hesitate with the ritual? Without my stakes and mallet, how am I going to complete it? Why Lord? I serve you as best I can. Why did you let this happen?*

The sudden screech of an owl, strident and close at hand, startled Gideon and yanked his attention back to his surroundings. A second angry screech shattered the silence, and he jumped a good foot. Looking up, he expected to see a large night bird. Instead, he discovered himself staring into the handsome smiling face of his nemesis. Highlighted by a stray beam of moonlight, the deceiver was comfortably seated on a large tree branch, just over head and less than fifteen feet away. Flawlessly dressed as always, his back pressed snuggly against the tree's trunk and he was fastidiously cleaning his nails.

"What are you doing here?" glared Gideon.

"Now, now, Mister Robinson, is that an acceptable way to greet your old friend? Our last chat left so much unsaid."

"I've nothing to say to you fiend!"

"My, oh my," sighed the good-looking apparition. "Always with you, it's, fiend this, or demon that! You really must work on your people skills. They're deplorable."

Gideon shifted his spear to both hands, and assumed a more aggressive stance. "Why don't you come down from there? Why don't you move a little closer?"

"Oh I'm fine right here, thank you; quite comfortable really. Tell me Gideon, do you ever wonder why you're the only one who sees me for what I am, that is to say, the only one who sees me at all?"

"God sees you! God, and those poor women you seduce!"

"Hmmm, God doesn't really count now, does he Robinson?" chuckled the monster. "And, as for the women, we'll never truly know, will we? We could ask some of them of course, but, oh that's right, you killed them all. Speaking of which, I think that earlier I was a bit hasty, there was probably more fun to be had with that cute waitress I gave you."

"What do you want?" snapped Gideon. "Why do you torment me?"

"You torment yourself. I'm just an old friend who enjoys our little chats together. After all we have so much in common you and me, the same hobbies; we're like two peas in a pod."

Gideon shook with rage. "Die deceiver!" he screamed. "Lord guide my wrath!" Moving adroitly, he shifted his spear to one hand, drew his arm back, and hurled the weapon with all his might. As the shaft flew straight and true, the demon leaned casually forward as if to examine a fleck of dust on his pant leg. Hurtling by, the spear missed him by a hair's breadth. Wasted, it whistled off into the dark.

Sitting back up as though nothing had occurred, the fiend nonchalantly glanced in the direction where Gideon's ineffectual missile had just disappeared. "Well, I guess we won't be seeing that for a long, long, while. Oh dear me, and it was your favorite wasn't it? I'm so sorry that you've lost your toy." At his own wry humor, the demon burst into a raucous fit of cackling laughter.

"You'll pay!" shrieked Gideon.

"Perhaps one day, but not right now; that account isn't due. Right now, let's you and I have some fun. I know where you've hidden the waitress," he grinned and winked. "I'll race you."

In a blur, the evil creature flitted off his branch and vanished into the night. Gideon howled, his every feature etched with anguish. *I have to get there first! The ritual isn't complete. I can't let him have her back.* With that thought, Gideon abandoned the shelter of the trees and began to sprint down the road.

Chapter 21

By the uncertain light of Claude's flashlight, Bobby Earl and Claude Archer slowly worked their way up the right side of Old Creek Road. Cautiously, they searched their way among the brush and trees that bordered the pavement. Other volunteers trailed behind them with swaying flashlights and lanterns. On the far side of the lane they could see lights and torches where Bud Fellers and the rest of the searchers were doing the same thing.

Claude paused and stared back into the darkness where others were falling behind. "I wish to hell that Doug had left his damn dogs at home," he complained. "They're not even trackers. They're just stupid mutts and they're slowing us down."

Bobby Earl looked back and could just make out one of the dogs, at the end of his leash, squatting by a bush. "Will you look at that," he groaned. "Doug has a bag and he's picking it up. Who the fuck cares! We're after the bastard that killed Janie and Marybeth and that idiot is stopping for dog shit!"

When Bobby turned back, Claude was pointing up the road. "What's that?" Something, maybe a hundred yards away, was flickering in and out of pools of moonlight."

Bobby's eyes were sharp. "Holy shit!" he exclaimed. "It's him! There he is! He's jogging up the road!"

"Hey! Hey! We see him!" screamed Claude.

"Get him!" yelled someone, and Claude and Bobby Earl left the brush for the pavement and charged off in pursuit.

Behind them frenzied pandemonium erupted among the searchers as everyone surged onto the road. Amid a chorus of shouts, two men with rifles opened an ineffectual fire, followed by a third with an out-of-range shotgun. Cracking booms echoed between the trees and brilliant muzzle flashes blinded anyone unlucky enough to be looking in the shooters' direction. By that time, several other men were chasing hot after Claude's and Bobby Earl's heels.

The rest of the mob also began to trot and from the back of the pack another shot rang out. That was followed by the angry sound of Bud Fellers' stentorian voice. "Stop the fucking shooting! No more shooting you morons! You'll hit our own guys."

"Get down there Bud," yelled Jean Rudolph just as loudly. "We want him alive. Don't let anyone do anything stupid." In response, Fellers, and a couple of others, picked up their pace, moving from a jog to a slow run.

Far in advance of the scrum, one of the chasers close to Bobby Earl stopped, drew a Glock pistol and loudly emptied his clip. The man they pursued zigzagged from side to side, but, apparently unscathed, he kept running. Watching the action, Fellers again picked up his pace.

"Don't kill him! Don't kill him!" yelled Corky Jones

The man ran hard. He didn't look back, and bit by bit, he started to pull away from the mob. Only Bobby Earl and Claude were still closing. Claude panted heavily. "We're going to fucking lose him," he gasped. "I can't keep this up." Bobby was winded too, but he'd been a star running back in high school, and he dug deep for one last burst of speed.

Fifteen feet away from the man, he skidded to a stop and hurled a heavy crescent wrench that he'd been carrying in his pocket.

The precisely machined chunk of flying metal struck the fugitive directly between his shoulder blades. With a scream of agony, he pitched forward onto the pavement. Before he could escape, Claude was on him, kicking again and again as the man writhed, squirming and moaning. "How do you like that you murdering piece of shit! Not so fun now, is it?"

"This is for Janie and Marybeth, you son of a bitch!" yelled Bobby Earl as he added his polished Tecovas Caimans to the assault.

Trotting up, Bud Fellers grabbed Claude by the shoulders and roughly pulled him back. "Stop it you two!" he commanded. "You're killing him!"

"Who gives a shit? Let me go!" raged Claude.

"Yeah," chimed in Bobby, who was now being restrained by others. "That monster killed Jane and Marybeth, and he cut their fucking heads off! Let's tear him to pieces!"

Meanwhile, Corky Jones leaned down, lifted the murderer by his belt and then flipped him over. "Oh! Jesus Christ!" he gasped.

"I can't see. I can't see. What is it? What's happening?" whined Kim Roberts, who'd abandoned his job at the motel and trailed along.

Jean Rudolph, standing next to Corky, looked down at the unconscious man. "It's not him!" she yelled, seething with anger. "What's going on here, you stupid assholes, is that we just tried to kill Clyde Carney from the feed store!"

Chapter 22

About half a mile away, the FBI's old Crown Vic slowly negotiated a sharp bend. Off in the distance, danced the bobbing lights of the coalition of the willing. "Look, there they are," exclaimed Leroy, pointing down the road.

Mickey sighed. "Whew, finally! I'd started to think this road was going to go on forever."

"I'm sorry Mickey," apologized Leroy, looking contrite. "I guess I forgot how long it takes."

"It's all right. It was a good idea. We didn't see anything, but at least we stopped at those farms and warned the people to be on their guard. The more folks who're watching out, the fewer places this guy will be able to hide."

Suddenly, Leroy grabbed excitedly at her arm. "Stop the car! Now, stop now!"

Mickey braked hard and pulled off the pavement. "What? What is it? Do you see something?"

Leroy pointed into the night. "Kill the lights! Over there, about two hundred yards! Up by the abandoned Peterson place, something bright; it moved pretty fast. I only saw it for a second, but... it looked like a man!"

In the ensuing darkness, they both stared in the direction Caderette had indicated. Squatting on a nearby hill, bathed in moonlight, stood a dilapidated old barn and the apparent remains of a derelict farm. As they watched, the man from room number eight at the motel ran out of a stand of trees. He loped along the crest of the hill, and then quickly ducked into the barn.

"Holy Shit!" gushed Mickey. "It's him! It's Smith! I saw him! Let's get after him!" Breathlessly, she grabbed the shotgun, released it from its dash clip, and threw open her door. "Come on," she urged. "Hurry."

Leroy also scrambled out of the car. "He's cornered. We'll get him this time."

Energized and excited, Mickey set a fast pace away from the road and was soon jogging up the slope toward the abandoned buildings. Leroy, several strides behind, worked hard to keep up. As they neared their goal, Mickey slowed and began to move more cautiously. Creeping, she edged up next to the wall of the old barn. Leroy joined her, bent over with his hands on his knees and panted softly.

Mickey listened carefully, but all she could hear was Leroy's quiet wheezing. Moving warily, she worked her way over to a small mullioned window. With extreme caution, she raised her head and quickly peeked. The barn was soot black inside and the window was filthy.

She turned to Leroy and shook her head. "I can't see anything," she whispered. "We'll have to risk the door."

"Ok, I'm ready," mouthed Leroy, still breathing heavily from his jog up the hill.

Looking determined, Mickey chambered a round into her shotgun, and began to creep along the wall. When she reached its end, for a split second, she stuck her head around the corner. Turning back to Leroy, she spoke softly. "It looks like the main door is our only way in or out, so we go through at the same time. I'll break left, you go right..."

"Is that my right or your right?" asked Leroy who had turned away from the barn.

Mickey glanced over her shoulder. "My right. Are you up for this, Leroy?"

Caderette straightened, turned around, and pulled his pistol from its holster. "I said I was; let's just do it." To Mickey, his voice sounded strained and nervous.

Both of them edged cautiously toward the barn's door which was more or less closed, but nevertheless ajar. Leroy leaned forward and pulled on its metal handle so that it swung outward with a jarring creak. Mickey and Leroy froze. Minutes seemed to slip by, but after the door's initial screech the silence was as profound as if the noise never occurred.

I'm supposed to be trained for this, thought Mickey. *I can do this*. Then, she gave Leroy a lets-do-it look and, crouched low, they both moved quickly and quietly through the opening and into the barn.

A dozen paces apart on either side of the door, they each huddled back next to the outside wall and strained to reconnoiter their surroundings. Air in the old structure tasted musty and metallic and the darkness inside felt thick and oppressive. Indistinct shapes of abandoned farm implements and other unidentifiable debris cluttered the derelict barn's interior. Visibility was no more than a couple of feet.

"Do you see anything?" whispered Mickey.

"Nothing, it's darker than a stack of black cats," whispered Leroy back. "Got your flashlight?"

"Yeah," continued Mickey, "but, if he's armed, it'll just make us a target. Let's wait a minute and see if our eyes will adjust." She continued in a louder voice meant to carry, "Mister Smith, this is the FBI! We have the barn surrounded. There's no way for you to escape. You need to put up your hands and come out where we can see you."

"I know who you are," echoed a tense reply from the recesses of the barn. "You're those two meddling officers from the motel. You shouldn't be here! I warned you. You can't help. You need to leave!"

"I understand Joe," cajoled Mickey, "but you and I both know that can't happen. You assaulted a federal officer. That won't go away, but right now, all we want to do is talk."

"It's not Joe," answered the disembodied voice. "It's Gideon, Gideon Robinson. You don't understand. You can't understand. I've been chosen. I'm the only one who can stop him."

"Then help us to understand, Mister Robinson," coaxed Leroy.

Hairs raised on the back of Gideon's neck and he glanced behind himself. Red eyes and shining pearly-whites flashed at him from the darkness. Looking calm and collected, the demon grinned and whispered, "It looks like the jigs finally up this time, Robinson old-boy. This is what comes of being too self-righteous. I told you, again and again, that you should leave well enough alone! Well now, your end is here and you've only yourself to blame."

Gideon stood with his back pressed against one of the barn's large rough support timbers and trembled. Blood drenched his clothes and his face was contorted in a grimace that might have been either anguish or rage. In his hands he clutched an old metal harvesting scythe. The tool's rusty metal blade dripped gore that pooled on the floor at his feet. "Go away! Just leave me alone!" he shouted.

"You know that we can't do that Mister Robinson," answered Mickey. Come out with your hands on your head and you'll be fine. This will all be over." Then, she caught Leroy's attention and pointed in the direction of Robinson's voice. Step by quiet step, she began to slink deeper into the inky shadows.

"Not you!" screamed Robinson. "Him! Him! He's here!"

"Who's here? Is there someone else with you?" asked Mickey, inadvertently revealing her new position.

Robinson's voice edged on hysteria as he again shouted, "Him! Him!"

"Him who?" answered Leroy.

"The demon you fools, the vampire!"

"Holy Shit!" muttered Leroy.

Mickey spoke in a soothing voice. "There is no vampire Mister Robinson. There's just you. We'll make sure that you're safe, but you need to come out right now."

"No he's real! I have to stop him!" Gideon screamed from the darkness. "I warned you not to get involved! You can't stay here. Your lives mean nothing against his destruction. If you stay here both of you are going to die!"

"No one has to die here," countered Leroy. "We can help you Mister Robinson. Just tell us where Gracie is?"

"You can't help! No one can help!"

Suddenly, howling a blood-curdling scream, Gideon charged from hiding. He clutched the rusty scythe held high above his head and stormed straight for Mickey. As the horrible apparition swept out of the darkness, she threw herself violently to one side.

Gideon swung his makeshift weapon with all his substantial might. Mickey struggled to bring up her heavy shotgun. In that instant, her feet tripped over something round. Off balance, her momentum carried her backwards. The onrushing scythe hissed through space where she'd only just stood. With a resounding "crash," it embedded itself into one the barn's timbers. Inches below the trapped blade, Mickey slammed into the same post. Gasping for breath, she continued her uncontrolled fall to the ground. Her face hit the dirt floor with an "Ooff!" and her shotgun rattled away out of reach.

Leroy heard Gideon's scream and noise from the subsequent commotion, but he couldn't see anything of what was occurring. "Mickey, are you all right?" he cried. "Turn on your light so that I can see you."

In the silence, Gideon wrestled with the scythe, but found he couldn't free it from the ancient timber's grip. "Don't abandon me Lord!" he yelled. "Give me your strength!"

A stunned Mickey heard Gideon close at hand, but she'd also heard Leroy's shout. Fumbling, she managed to flick on her flashlight. From her vantage point in the dirt, the sudden burst of light illuminated a floor covered with blood and Gracie Young's gore splattered legs tied together with a thick rope. Mickey's eyes went wide. She turned her face in what she thought was Leroy's direction. A foot from her nose, she stared into the dead lifeless eyes of Gracie's severed head. Mickey stared at the head and then looked at her own hands and arms. *I'm lying in her blood!* Mickey's eyes rolled back into her head, she sagged, and then her prostrate body began to convulse.

Gideon, glanced down at the twitching FBI woman and gave up trying to free the scythe. Instead, he reached down to retrieve her shotgun. As he straightened, the other officer slipped from the shadows.

"Pickle's Forge Police! Drop the gun!"

Gideon stepped back. A pool of light flowed from Mickey's dropped flashlight. On either side, just beyond the pool's darkening edges, the two men faced each other. Leroy could see that Robinson held the shotgun pointed toward the floor. Also muzzle down, he held his own weapon firmly at his side.

"You fat meddling idiot!" screeched Robinson. "You don't know what you're doing. He's deceived you!"

"Drop the shotgun!"

"Only the righteous can stop him, only the chosen!"

Leroy stared at Mickey's now still body lying, next to Gracie's head, bathed in the light and blood. *He's bat-shit crazy!* he thought. "Mister Robinson,

I'm going to count to three and, if you don't put down the shotgun, I'm going to start shooting. One... Two..."

Outside in the moonlight, Jean Rudolph, Bud Fellers, and Bobby Earl were at the front of the posse which had cautiously worked its way up the hill and approached the barn.

"What do you think Bud?" asked Jean. "With their car down there on the road, I don't see where else they could have gone."

"Yeah, but I don't see 'em. If they're here, they must be inside."

"Hey, look, I think I see a light," blurted Bobby Earl.

Everyone turned toward the barn's small window. Dim, but still visible, the faintest of glows emanated from somewhere deep behind the dirty glass panes. Bobby stepped closer. Before he reached it, the window exploded from its frame. Shattered splinters of wood and shards of glass ripped through the air, hurled violently outward by a load of double-aught buckshot.

Flash after flash lit the gaping hole as, almost continuous, repeated reports of a shotgun and a pistol echoed out into the night. Then, just as suddenly as it began, the storm ended. Raising shakily to his feet from where he'd flung himself onto the ground, Bobby stared in awe at the now dark opening. "God Damn!" he whispered.

"Come on," urged Fellers, gripping his own pistol. Resolutely, he stalked toward the barn's door closely followed by the other vigilantes. The old door hung partially open, and Bud paused a dozen feet away. The rest of the crowd clutching their weapons, torches, and lanterns formed a loose half circle just behind him.

"What do you think?" questioned Claude. "Should we go in?"

At that exact moment, a tall muscular man staggered out of the opening and came to an abrupt halt. Blood drenched his clothes. Gunshot wounds punctured his left shoulder and his right thigh. Everything went utterly quiet as, motionless, the startled man and mob stared at one another in unexpected surprise."

"It's him!" shrieked Kim Roberts from the back of the mob. "That's Smith!"

For another split second, frozen in time, everyone continued to stand and stare. Then, the stillness broke. The man extended his bloody hands like claws, bellowed a scream resounding of anguish and insanity, and rushed forward. Roaring in response, the coalition of the willing surged headlong to meet him. For a moment, the wounded man held his own, grappling with those nearest and forcing his way through the press. As more people closed in, he faltered. Suddenly, he went down under a rain of blows.

At the center of the furious brawl Carol Green raised her pitchfork. "This is for Mary Beth you son of a bitch!" she screeched. She shoved down hard on the tines and leaned on the handle. Instantly, the struggle stopped. Appalled, the crowd took an uncertain step back. The man lay pinned to the ground; the fork quivered in his chest.

Gideon, stared about himself with wide dying eyes. Just beyond the gawking ring of people, the demon slouched insolently against the barn and silently laughed. As his life slipped away, Gideon managed to stretch out a bloody arm and point. "Him!"

With a final rattling gasp, the man jerked once and died. Jean Rudolph turned and looked where he'd pointed. Nothing was there.

Chapter 23

The small lawn that bordered the Pickle's Forge city hall seemed to revel in the day's bright sunshine. Uncharacteristically, the curb in front of the building was packed with a mix of private and official looking cars. One, a late-model van, sported the words "County Coroner" in large black letters on its sides. Another similarly labeled van had just pulled away carrying a cargo that included four frozen bundles, wrapped in black plastic. The steaming bundles had been carefully removed from an ice box decorated with smiling penguins gussied up in red wool caps.

Almost as soon as that coroner's van left the curb, a silver sedan, with "State Trooper" lettered on its fenders, had quickly occupied the empty space. The sedan also sported the Oregon State Police's five-pointed star logo and the motto, "Honor, Loyalty, Dedication, Compassion and Integrity." Two uniformed officers, opened the patrol car's doors, climbed out, and walked purposefully toward the hall's concrete steps. At the top of the stairs, just out of earshot, FBI Agent in Charge, Steve Smallwood, and one of his subordinates were engaged in a conversation with Bud Fellers.

"Hiya Steve, Ernie," greeted one of the staties as they approached. "It looks like we missed a real ball twister on this one."

"Hi Burt; yeah it was pretty ugly," answered Smallwood.

"We hear that your gal did all right though," answered Burt. "You guys know Glen here don't you?"

"Sure we've met, hi Glen," chimed the second FBI agent.

Steve Smallwood placed a hand on Bud's shoulder. "Gentlemen, this is Bud Fellers. He's on the town council." Both uniformed officers stepped forward and shook Fellers' hand.

"Pleased to meet you Mister Fellers," intoned Glen. "We're sorry it couldn't have been under better circumstances. The state police want your whole town to know how hard we tried to get here sooner."

"We'll it's all over now," averred Bud. "We just appreciate the support that everyone's showing us."

"So Steve," probed Burt, "the scuttlebutt going around is that, after your agent lost her partner, she went toe to toe with the psycho and shot it out like the OK Corral?"

Smallwood hesitated. "Well ..."

Before he could continue, Bud Fellers broke in, busting with pride. "It wasn't Agent Butters that did him. She'd passed out. It was our own Pickle's Forge deputy, Leroy Caderette, who turned the tide on that animal!"

Each of the state troopers looked quizzically at Smallwood, and the Agent in Charge, shrugged.

"Come on inside boys," said Fellers, still enjoying the moment. "I'll introduce you to the man of the hour." All five men walked into the City Hall and Fellers closed the door behind them.

Later that day, the sun had begun to set and the scrum of vehicles no longer clogged the parking spaces in front of the city hall. Except for Jean Rudolph's Volvo and the venerable Crown Vic that brought Mickey and Edgar to town, the street was empty.

Leroy, his left arm bandaged and in a sling, led the way, followed by Mickey and Jean as they exited the old building and walked out to the curb. As they reached the sidewalk, they turned and faced one another. "Well Mickey, I guess this is it," he grinned.

"I don't know what to say Leroy," she sputtered. "I blew it, left you in the lurch, and you saved the day. Hell, you saved my life." Then, she turned to Major Rudolph. "Jean, Pickle's Forge has a damn good man here. They don't come much better."

"Don't I know it," she answered. "Bud and I have both asked Leroy to take over for Buzz."

"No kidding," smiled Mickey. "You're doing the right thing." Then, she turned back to Leroy. "Congratulations, Chief!"

"Chief? Yeah chief; it's the first time someone's called me that. I think I'm gonna like it."

"I'm sorry I let everyone down," apologized Mickey. "I guess I just wasn't cut out for any of this."

"Nonsense Agent Butters," retorted Jean, you're a skilled person too. Every one of us here in Pickle's Forge knows that. We'd never have made it through this nightmare without you."

"Jean's right Mickey," added Leroy. "Don't beat yourself up. What's done is done. As far as I'm concerned, you're still the pro and you never let me down even for a second!"

"So what happens for you now?" asked Jean.

"Honestly I don't know," sighed Mickey. "For now, I go back to Portland and take it one day at a time. The FBI doesn't take kindly to agents who lie on their application. If I'm lucky, I go back to cybercrime and stay in the office. If not, well there's always waitressing."

"Mickey, I'm the mayor of Pickle's Forge," laughed Jean. "If you ever want to be a volunteer deputy on our police force, the job's yours."

Mickey smiled, gave Jean and Leroy big hugs. Then she walked over to the Crown Vic and opened the driver's door. Before she could slide in, Leroy called out. "If the waitress thing doesn't pan out, I'm holding you to the deputy job."

"Any time Mickey, it's yours," chimed Jean.

Leroy and Jean stood at the curb smiling until long after the Crown Vic had dwindled into the distance.

Mickey received a commendation for valor from the FBI, but was then quietly and sternly instructed to resign. The waitress thing didn't pan out, but when she approached LockCell about the possibility of returning to her old job, company executives nearly wet themselves with excitement. They'd been sorry to lose her in the first place, and now they could legitimately claim that one of their star cyber security professionals was an ex-FBI agent with a citation for bravery.

After signing their contract, Mickey eschewed a social life and pressed her nose firmly to the grindstone. Her subsequent rise within the company, could safely be described as meteoric. Twenty-seven months of long days after she drove away from Pickle's Forge, she was seated behind a costly walnut desk, in a large corner office with expansive views out of its embarrassingly large picture windows. The desk held a variety of the best and most expensive tech that money could buy, and mounted on the office door was an engraved plaque that read, "Kitrina Kathleen Butters, Chief Security Officer."

Mickey was just polishing off the last bites of another, eaten-at-her desk, fast-food lunch, when her secretary knocked lightly on the door, and stepped in. "Hi Kevin," said Mickey around a mouthful of French fries, "what's up?"

"A special delivery letter just arrived for you Miss Butters. It looks official so I thought I better bring it right in."

"Thank you," said Mickey, wiping her hands on a paper napkin and reaching out to accept the proffered letter. After Kevin left, she scrutinized the envelope. It was indeed a special delivery, and it was addressed to Ms. Kitrina Butters, in care of LockCell. The return was an Oregon State Police address complete with a small embossed OSP seal.

Curious and a little bemused, she slit the envelope and shook its contents on to her desk. What fell out was a photograph and a handwritten note on official letterhead. She picked up the note first.

"Dear Mickey," it read. "I'm going to be in town for a few days, starting on the 12th. I'm coming for a law enforcement workshop, but I'm going to have some free time. I think about you often and feel like we had a connection. If you're interested I'd like to take you out for dinner. Leroy." A phone number was written under his name.

Smiling, she turned over the photo, which had landed facedown. Smiling back at her was Leroy Caderette, twenty pounds lighter, smartly dressed in a State Police uniform, and wearing a Smokey-the-Bear hat. Mickey stared at the picture. *Why the hell not?* she thought, and reached for her phone.

Chapter 24

On regular days, Rachel didn't much like her work. She truly fucking hated it on Wednesdays. The job at the department store cosmetics counter already sucked big time; eight hours a day, five days a week, spritzing cheap old ladies with stinky shit that no self-respecting millennial would ever buy. Wednesdays were even worse. On Wednesdays the department store stayed open until midnight, and Rachel was expected to work her counter until the very last biddy, jonesing for free perfume, finally left. That was a bummer, but what really made Wednesdays a shit-show was her long commute home. She felt that DC's subways were passable during normal hours, but late at night she totally detested them.

So far, this Wednesday had gone better than most. Dashing out of the store, she'd managed to catch a train on the Green Line almost immediately. At Gallery Place, she had to change to the Red Line which required a time-consuming trek across the cavernous station. Late at night when the place was mostly deserted the long walk always gave her the willies. Tonight, had been quieter than usual. She'd reached the Red Line without incident, and her wait on the empty platform had been a short one.

When she'd boarded, she'd been nervous that she would either have to stand or, worse yet, sit down next to some creep. The ride on the Red Line from Gallery Place all the way out to Forest Glen, where she parked her car, was the longest segment of Rachel's commute. It was also the segment when she was most likely to attract unwanted attention. "Yes!" she'd mouthed and pumped her fist when she spotted the two empty, forward-facing, seats.

The car was one of the funky, Italian made, Breda models that were soon to be retired, and the old carriage accommodated far fewer passengers than newer sorts. As the train made stops at Judiciary Square, Union Station, NoMa-Gallaudet U, and Rhode Island Avenue, the car slowly filled. Thankfully, the seat next to Rachel stayed empty.

When the car's doors opened at Brookland Station, it looked like that was about to change. A man staggered aboard, obviously intoxicated. The filthy clothes he wore looked like they hadn't been washed in a month, if ever. The drunk looked blearily around and then focused on the empty seat. *Oh no!* thought Rachel. *Oh fuck no!* She was about to jump up, when someone spoke softly from just behind her shoulder.

"Excuse me miss. Is this seat taken?"

Turning to look, she saw a man that she hadn't noticed come on board. The stranger, perhaps thirty, was blond, handsome, and very well dressed. Rachel glanced back at the approaching drunk. "No it's not. Please sit," she encouraged sliding over.

The man adjusted his elegant cashmere coat and eased into the empty seat. "Thank you," he smiled. "I feel lucky."

Rachel stared into his eyes. *My God! His eyes are beautiful. He's beautiful! I could lose myself in those eyes.*

END

About the Author

Igrew up in Santa Paula, California, "Citrus Capital of the World." After graduating high school, I attended the University of California at Riverside, California State University Humboldt, and Lane Community College in Eugene, Oregon. Over the years, I've worked a variety of different jobs: stock clerk, farm laborer, janitor, pot washer, computer programmer, bicycle mechanic, systems analyst, agricultural inspector, information systems administrator, and probably a couple that I've forgotten. Today, I'm happily married and live and write in Prescott, Arizona.

Please visit my Author's Website at donaldhealey.com for FREE extras and information about my other books.

Thank you for being one of my readers!